ASHES IN A TEARDROP

A STANISLAUS COUNTY COMMUNITY NOVEL

QUERCUS REVIEW PRESS
MODESTO, CA
2014

Published by Quercus Review Press
Department of English
Modesto Junior College
quercusreviewpress.com

With the support of The Stanislaus Library Foundation

Cover illustration by Jasbinder Kaur Atwal
Author photos by Brian Lillie

First Printing
Printed in the United States of America

Printed on acid-free paper
10 9 8 7 6 5 4 3 2 1

ISBN-13: 978-0692272015
ISBN-10: 0692272011

Proceeds from the sale of this book benefit the Stanislaus Library
Foundation and Quercus Review Press' creative writing scholarships
at Modesto Junior College.

CONTENTS

PREFACE & ACKNOWLEDGMENTS

This story begins when a young couple, biking along the Tuolumne River, discovers an abandoned teardrop trailer on the riverbank, made visible by the low water level, a result of the current drought. Readers will recognize local landmarks and real-life historical figures, as the story unfolds. *Ashes in a Teardrop* will take readers on an adventure of suspense and intrigue throughout Stanislaus County.

But that's not where the *real* story begins. The real story begins with a great idea, a lofty goal, a passion for literacy, and a community of amazing volunteers.

Ashes in a Teardrop, Stanislaus County's first community novel, is the collective work of 15 local authors. It was modeled after the community novel project of the Topeka & Shawnee County Public Library in Kansas. In Stanislaus County, this project grew into a community-wide collaborative effort. A lively brainstorming session, facilitated by volunteer, Marian Martino, in January 2014, led to the basic premise of the mystery, set in Stanislaus County.

At the conclusion of the first meeting, it became apparent that this would become a true collaboration – not just a collective work. The original plan called for one brainstorming meeting, with each consecutive author independently writing his or her chapter based on the previous author's work. However, the group chose to meet periodically to continue developing the ideas together.

The book was edited one chapter at a time by Clare Noonan, a former writer and editor at *The Modesto Bee*. As each chapter was edited, it was also recorded with narration provided by Emerson Drake, who also volunteered his time and talent. Beginning April 15, during National Library Week, one chapter per week was published on the library website in print and audio formats.

With the final phase of this project, the collaborative continued to grow. The Stanislaus Library Foundation, in cooperation with Quercus Review Press (affiliated with Modesto Junior College), facilitated the printing of the bound version of *Ashes in a Teardrop*. Professor of English at Modesto Junior College, Sam Pierstorff, provided the layout and design, and he enlisted the help of several colleagues for the final proofing: Jennifer Hamilton, Jason Wholstadter, Barbara Jensen, JoAnn Melo, Shelley Circle, Optimism One, Pamela Kopitzke, Amanda Heinrichs, Dimitri Keriotis, Beverley Steichen, Susan Cassidy, Jillian Daly, Bruce Anders, Sara Berger, Tara Bates, and Michael Akard.

The art of Jasbinder Kaur Singh, whose work was selected from a countywide art contest, was incorporated into the cover design. Local art teachers

Lori Kramer, Henrietta Sparkman and Sandy Veneman contributed by serving as art contest judges.

Library staff, including Michael Mayreis, Kelly Ferrini, John Fleming, Jason Phillips, Sheri Darrough, Amy Taylor, Laura Ferrell, Brian Lillie and Susan Lilly contributed to the project in the areas of planning, coordinating authors, recording/editing, marketing, web design and photography.

Any new project has the potential for unintended consequences, a term usually associated with negative outcomes. In this case, however, the consequences became welcome surprises. New partnerships were formed between the Library, Stanislaus Library Foundation, Modesto Junior College, Quercus Review Press, and numerous individuals.

The community novel created opportunities for aspiring authors to enhance their creative writing skills. It offered more experienced writers a chance to mentor others. It engaged a community of writers to work toward a common goal. The result is a novel, set against the familiar backdrop of Stanislaus County, written *by* our community *for* our community.

Proceeds from the sale of this book will benefit the Stanislaus Library Foundation, which provides funds for vital library programs, and Quercus Review Press, to help support creative writing scholarships and future local publishing projects such as this.

We hope you enjoy this truly collaborative novel as much as we enjoyed putting it together for you.

ASHES IN A TEARDROP

A STANISLAUS COUNTY COMMUNITY NOVEL

CHAPTER ONE
Micheal Maxwell

"Come on, slowpoke!" Amy Curtis shouted over her shoulder, her flaxen ponytail bobbing up and down as her husband struggled behind her.

"Where's the fire?" Jerry grunted between his pedaling and labored gasps for air.

All he could hear was his wife's laughter as she rounded the curve, widening the gap between them even farther. I didn't want to come on this stupid bike ride in the first place, he thought. Yes, I'm overweight, and yes, Amy looks terrific after her diet, but did she have to pick the hottest day of the year for a bike ride?

Jerry rolled to a stop. "It's over 100 degrees out here," he muttered. He took a gulp of water from his plastic bottle. The water was so hot it would have made a great cup of tea. The hot water just added to his frustration. Jerry spit it onto the steaming asphalt.

"Where the heck did you go?" he yelled down the trail. "What about quality time together, huh? What about that?"

Forty minutes on the trail and they hadn't seen a soul. The river was more like a brook without any babble. Jerry was hot, sweaty, chafed and more than ready to head back to the car. Home was a half-hour drive across Modesto. There's a Mickey D's on Oakdale Road. I could get a mocha frappe. The thought calmed Jerry a bit.

"This just isn't working," he said softly as he laid his bike down. "I wish I'd bought the big-butt seat. Who cares if it looks silly?" Jerry kicked the dust as he moved to sit on a chunk of log. "I'm in pain here!" His cry for sympathy went unheard.

"Legion Park," he mused. "I thought parks had grass and water and stuff. This river is practically dried up. The grass is dead. Drought killed it all and I'm next. Now I'm sitting on a stump talking to myself!"

Jerry bent down and picked up a rock about the size of a walnut and hurled it at the bushes. Kurr-thunk! The rock hit something that definitely wasn't wood. He ran his fingers over the hot, dusty sand at his feet. A rock a bit smaller than the first was just below the surface. He tried to throw close to where the first one had landed.

The rock hit metal. Jerry slowly lifted his aching body off the log. He stretched and strained to see what was beyond the brush. Curiosity getting the better of him, he crossed the path and peeked through the dead and dying bushes.

A glint of light flashed between the dry leaves of a dusty oleander. Jerry pushed back branches, trying to get a look at what lay beyond. The vegetation cracked, snapped and broke in his hands. He looked around. No Amy to tell him not to. Nobody else, period. He started tearing limbs out of the way. They were so dry that there was little resistance. As Jerry stomped on a low-lying branch, he saw another flash of light.

He fought his way through the vegetation. His sweaty T-shirt caught on a sharp spike and tore. He swore beneath his breath but kept plowing deeper into the brush.

Then he saw it. Ensnared in a web of broken limbs, wire, clumps of river algae and several inches of dirt was an old-fashioned teardrop trailer. It rested at a 45-degree angle, supported by branches and completely hidden from the bike trail. On the other side of the river was a steep embankment and open field.

"How did you get here?" Jerry said, panting as he continued clearing a path. "This is so cool! It's just like the ones at the MJC Graffiti Car Show."

He inched down the side of the trailer and made his way to the back. The bank was dry and the water was at least 20 feet below, but the angle was steep. It was obvious from the amount of debris tangled on and around the trailer that it had been submerged at one time. A torn corner of a license plate was all that was left of the small metal frame on the bumper.

No license, no ID, Jerry thought. His mind raced with visions of the little trailer polished, shining like a new nickel and being towed behind a 1950 Ford Woody station wagon. He imagined Amy coming out of a mountain lake in a bright red bathing suit just the color of their wagon. The fact that they didn't have a Woody was not important at the moment. Jerry's mind was spinning, trying to figure out how he was going to get the trailer off this riverbank and home.

"Jerry!" Amy's voice cut through his thoughts. "Jerry! Where are you?" She sounded panicky.

"Over here!" Jerry yelled.

"Over where?"

"Hold on," he called.

"Were you watering the bushes?" Amy asked with a giggle.

"No!" Jerry said indignantly as he appeared through the brush.

"Look at you! You're bleeding."

Jerry looked down at his torn shirt. His legs stung from scrapes and scratches. The abrasions on his arms completed the set. "I'm fine. Listen."

"You need to get those cleaned up," Amy said. "Did you fall? Why'd you stop?"

"Would you just listen?" Jerry said.

"What?" Amy asked, a bit taken aback by her husband's tone.

"I found a trailer! It is so cool. A little teardrop trailer like the ones we saw at the car show at MJC. Remember, you said how cute they were? I found one!"

"How did you get on Craigslist out here?"

"No, no, no. I found one over there!" Jerry said, pointing toward the gap in the bushes. "Come look."

"I do not want to look like I've been clawed by a

bobcat," Amy said.

"Then give me your phone," Jerry said, motioning with his fingers.

Amy handed him the phone. "Who are you going to call?"

Jerry quickly tapped numbers into the phone. "Mario, it's Jerry. I need your help." He paused, then said, "Doing what? Bring her with you. You got a car seat, don'tcha? Look, I found an old-fashioned aluminum teardrop trailer. I need you to bring your flatbed trailer so I can get it home. No, I don't have a hitch. Besides, I think the tires are flat."

"Are you crazy?" Amy huffed. "You can't just haul off a trailer."

Jerry gave her the "be quiet" wave and continued. "Just come out Yosemite, turn on Santa Cruz and keep going. Stop when it turns into Tioga. Yeah, yeah, way out. I don't know, 15, 20 minutes maybe." Jerry took a deep breath. "Yeah, yeah, east end of Legion Park. I'll be in the little parking lot. Awesome."

"You're going to jail!" Amy exclaimed, her eyes wide.

"OK! Thanks, buddy. See you soon," Jerry said, handing the phone back with a big smile.

"Are you nuts? You can't do this," Amy said. "It belongs to somebody. It's like grand theft auto without the auto. You'll get arrested. Honey, please. I know you're excited, but step back for a second. Think for a second. Here," she thrust out the phone. "Call Mario back and tell him you had a heat stroke or something. You were delirious."

"Listen, listen, listen. It's fine," Jerry said. "There's no license plate. It's been down there forever."

"It's fine, officer. It didn't have a license," Amy said, attempting a deep voice.

"You'll love it," Jerry answered. "It's awesome. I'll fix it all up and we can go camping."

"You hate camping."

"Can't I just take it home then figure it out?" Jerry's last defense was pleading.

"Remember the puppy you found?" Amy asked. "This will be like the puppy."

"No, no, I don't have to feed this, just clean it up."

"I give up," she sighed.

"Then I can take it home?"

"I didn't say that. I said, 'I give up.' If you and Mario want to go to jail and have little Bianca be turned over to Child Protective Services, that's up to you. I'm going home. It's hot out here and I do not intend to get arrested."

"OK, OK, I'll wait here for Mario," Jerry said. He picked up his bicycle and started riding back to the car. About 10 yards up the trail, he turned around and rode back to the log. He jumped off his bike and rolled the log to the middle of the trail.

"Now what?" Amy shouted. "You'll get somebody killed."

"We're the only ones dumb enough to be on this

trail in the middle of August," Jerry answered.

* * *

He watched the bikes' wheels spin on the bike rack as Amy drove away. Even under the shade of a tree, Modesto's mid-August heat was stifling. Leaning back against the Mary E. Grogan Grove sign at the edge of the grass, Jerry realized that Amy had taken the cell phone.

Nearly 30 minutes later, Mario pulled into the parking lot in his gigantic Cummins diesel pickup. Behind it was a lowboy trailer, complete with winch.

"Yes!" Jerry yelled, pumping his fist as he ran to the truck.

"So where's this trailer?" Mario asked, giving Jerry his famous what-kind-of mischief-are-we-about-to-get-into smile.

The pair had become friends when they attended Somerset Junior High. All through high school and junior college they had fought each other's battles and developed reputations for getting into crazy predicaments. Today seemed like a return to form.

"Down the trail about a mile," Jerry motioned.

"How am I supposed to get in there?" Mario asked. "There's cement posts everywhere."

"Not everywhere." Jerry pointed at a gap near the end of the line of white concrete posts.

"Well, let's go get it!" Mario was so excited that he sounded more like a teenager than a 34-year-old man. He dropped the truck into gear.

Jerry pulled himself into the front seat and shivered. "Man, this air-con really works," he said as the truck pulled onto the trail.

"New Freon," Mario said. "Did it myself and I added a bit extra. Works good, huh?"

"Where's the baby?" Jerry asked, looking into the rear seat.

"Tracy came home just as I was walking out the door. She asked what we were up to. I said salvaging. Good one, huh?"

"I'm using that one on Amy. OK, slow down a bit. I rolled a log onto the path. You should see it any ..." Jerry broke off for a long moment. "There it is!"

"What were you guys doing out here? It is insane hot today." Mario tapped the digital thermometer overhead. "103!"

"Amy said we'd burn up fat," Jerry said as he hopped out of the truck.

"More like you'd burn up!" Mario said with a laugh.

Jerry pushed the log to the side of the trail. Mario came and stood next to him.

"It's down there at kind of an angle," Jerry said. "Must have been there forever. The hitch is at this end."

"I'm gonna pull up farther," Mario said, looking

at the opening in the bushes. "We'll just pull 'er out and onto the flatbed. Can you get down to the hitch?"

"No problem," Jerry answered. "Can a winch pull out something that big?"

"Guaranteed to four tons!"

Jerry ran ahead of the truck and guided his friend until the back of the trailer was even with the teardrop. Mario cranked the wheel and backed his flatbed to match the angle of the little trailer. He jumped out with the truck idling.

Mario slipped on a pair of leather gloves stashed behind the winch, threw a switch and unrolled about 10 feet of cable. He hit the switch again, then took off the gloves and tossed them to Jerry.

"OK, loop the hook through the hitch bar and then hook it on the cable. Make sure the point is down. Got it?"

"Aye, aye, Cap'n." Jerry gave a sloppy salute.

He approached the trailer from a different angle this time. The triangle-shaped bars were snarled with vines, weeds and wire. Jerry shoved the hook though the debris and fixed it on the cable.

"Got it!" he yelled.

"Get out of the way!"

Jerry scrambled back up to the truck. The slack slowly lessened as Mario began reeling in the cable. As it came taut, the trailer broke its bonds of soil and branches and tore free. Foot by foot, yard by yard, the cable wound around the winch spool. Finally, the hitch appeared through the vegetation, providing the first full view of the aluminum teardrop.

"There she is! There she is!" Jerry yelled, raising his fist over his head as he did a victory dance.

Mario stopped the winch and hit a large black button on the side of his trailer. The back end of the lowboy tilted until it touched the ground. Pulling the winch lever again, the teardrop half rolled and half slid onto the flatbed.

"There you go, Jer!" Mario said, beaming at his friend. "Not bad. Not bad at all."

The two men stood and marveled at the tiny teardrop resting level and safe on the trailer. Jerry tried to open the door.

"Stuck."

Come on, Hulk. Give it some muscle," Mario teased.

The handle creaked. Jerry put his other hand above the door and pulled. The door made a sound like a vacuum-packed can of nuts and swung open. Jerry jumped back as two cans of pork and beans rolled out.

"Look at all the stuff!"

"There'll be time for exploring when we get this thing to your house," Mario said. "We probably should get out of here, don't you think?"

"Yeah, let's go."

It took nearly an hour to secure the trailer and drive to Jerry's house. As they backed it into the driveway, Amy came out the front door.

"And where do you think that is going?" she asked.

"Where I can work on it in the shade," Jerry said, guiding Mario to the open garage.

"And my car will go where?"

"On the drive?"

"Great," Amy said. "So I can blister my butt every time I get in?"

"Not at night or in the morning," Jerry said meekly.

"Grrrrrrr; you two!" She stomped into the house and slammed the door.

"I gotta get home," Mario said. "I promised Tracy I'd barbecue some chicken tonight."

"Thanks, buddy. I owe you one." Jerry patted his friend on the shoulder.

"More like a hundred."

"What?" Jerry asked.

"Nuthin'," Mario said with a laugh as he got into the truck.

After an hour's work, the Shop-Vac had collected almost a gallon of dust off the trailer. Jerry had washed his new treasure and was just about to polish it when Amy stepped into the garage, wiping her hands on a kitchen towel.

"Need some help?" she asked sheepishly.

"Excuse me? Who are you and what have you done with my wife?" Jerry said with mock severity.

"It really is cute, sweetie," Amy said, crossing the garage and giving Jerry a peck on the cheek.

Knowing this was as close to an apology as he was going to get, Jerry beamed with childlike pleasure at finally having an accomplice in the Great Teardrop Trailer Caper. "I was about to start polishing her up. It is stuffed with who knows what. How would you like to figure out what to keep and what to throw away?"

"Is it nasty inside?"

"No, it is really tight, so there's almost no water damage," he said. "It kind of whooshed when I finally got the door open. I'll go get the garbage can for you."

Amy peered inside the trailer. She was amazed to see stacks of papers, canned goods and clothes. They looked like they'd been tumbled in a clothes dryer. The surprising thing was that there was no smell of mold or mildew. She pulled out a stack of magazines and newspapers that sat near the door. Dry as a bone.

"These are all dated 1997," Amy said, holding them up to show Jerry.

"Cool. Here you go, recycle and garbage," he said, tossing back the lids of the bins.

Amy dropped a handful of papers in the recycle bin and Jerry started his polishing.

The cans were nearly full before Amy was able to get inside the trailer. She stacked some usable things — pots and pans, silverware, an ice chest and some men's clothing — on the garage floor.

There was a small bench seat and a fold-up table attached to the wall of the trailer. Amy sat on the bench and looked around the tiny space. There were a pair of accordion doors toward the front.

Must be the bed, she thought, moving half crouched across the space. Behind the doors there was a small mattress and a jumble of blankets and pillows. A hand-stitched quilt caught her eye. She gave a tug, but it didn't budge. As she pulled at the quilt again, she realized something was rolled up in it.

A heavy enameled vase. Amy stepped out of the trailer to see it in better light.

"Jerry," Amy called softly.

"Once I get this all buffed out it is going to look amazing," he said with pride.

"Jerry, honey."

Amy moved to the rear of the trailer and held the vase at arm's length. The couple paused for a long moment, gazing at the beautiful colors and unusual shape of the vessel.

"Isn't it gorgeous?" Amy said.

"What is it?"

"I don't know. But the lid is sealed with red wax. Look."

CHAPTER TWO

Kent Johnson

"Kind of looks like a giant mother-of-pearl Parcheesi piece." Jerry rubbed his fingers over the smooth enameled surface at the base of the vase. His fingers touched the wax line and continued to the bulbous cap that sat atop the small spire-like neck.

"It's too heavy for me to keep holding up," Amy said and put it on the trailer floor.

Jerry picked up the vase and rotated it in his hands. "I wonder what this has in it. Feels like about 6 pounds," he said. "Red wax seal means whatever it is has been untouched by air."

He carried the vase back to the fold-up table, hunched over to protect his head from the low ceiling. Amy followed him.

"Maybe it's some rare liquor that's well aged. Wine, maybe. We might be able to sell it at an auction and make a tidy sum from one of those collectors," Amy said, brushing a strand of hair from her face with the back of her dusty hand.

"I don't think so." Jerry looked at the bottom of the vessel, which had "CB Memorial Home" neatly handwritten in blue ink. "It says it came from a memorial home. Probably someone's ashes."

"Ew, it's a body?" Amy asked, taking a step back.

"That's my guess," Jerry said, spinning the urn around again. "Look at this." He pointed at the wax covering the lid.

"What?"

"It has an embossing."

"A what?" Amy moved in and looked closely at the seal.

"Like they used on envelopes in the old days so you could see if anyone opened your mail," Jerry said. "They pressed your initials, a monogram, family crest or whatever into the melted wax at the seal line. My dad had one of those kits from the '60's." He squinted and moved the urn to get the best light on the embossing.

"Looks like two R's in a mirror image," Amy said.

"Yeah, I wonder if it's someone's initials?" Jerry asked. "I've seen that somewhere before, though."

"Sure you have, Jer. Maybe you were at the services. What I do know is that your little project has an unidentified body involved with it. I think you need to call the Sheriff's Department."

"Why? I mean, no one's seemed to miss him since 1997."

"Or her," Amy said. "How would you like it if it was a relative of yours and some stranger had the remains?"

"If it was my crazy Uncle Lewis, more power to 'em."

"Seriously," she said.

"Maybe we can just take the urn to the coroner's office?"

"How do you explain where you got it?" Amy asked. "Come on, do the right thing. Call the sheriff out and give them the details."

"But what if they take my trailer?" Jerry touched the inside wall.

"That won't be the last teardrop you shed."

"That was bad, Amy," he said, putting the urn back on the floor against a magazine rack. He stared at it and shook his head. "You're probably right. I'll go in and call the Sheriff's Department and tell them the whole story."

"I didn't say you had to do it this instant. I mean, we can explore a little more," Amy continued with a mischievous smile.

Jerry returned her grin and nodded his head.

Amy pointed toward the bed where the urn had been. "You take the front and I'll take the back."

Her eyes darted to the urn, then to the magazine rack. She pulled a paperback out and scanned the cover of John Grisham's "The Firm." She pulled out three more Grisham novels and set them on the table.

"Guy seems to be fascinated with the law," Amy

yelled. "Four books by Grisham."

She found Sunset magazines from 1995, 1996 and 1997, with no address labels. Amy scanned the contents, hoping to find a common theme, but no luck.

"I remember now," Jerry called from the front.

"Remember what?"

"Hold on, let me..." He wrenched his body around, trying to get out of the little sleeping space. "Ouch," Jerry said, as his head hit the ceiling. The quilt the urn had been found in twisted around him. His feet got tangled up and he fell on the floor with a thud.

"Remember what?" Amy asked again.

"I said just a minute." Jerry rubbed his head and looked at his hand. He pulled the quilt from his legs and crawled to the back of the trailer with Amy.

"Did you find anything up there?"

"No," he said, "but I remember where I saw that embossing." He grinned at her like he had won the lottery.

"Where?" Amy asked, one hand tapping a Sunset magazine.

"The H Bar B," Jerry said.

"The what?"

"The H Bar B in Oakdale." Jerry's head tilted to the side as he looked into Amy's eyes.

"What are you talking about?"

"It's an old cowboy bar. Been around forever," Jerry explained.

"So? What, the R and R stands for Rob Roy, a favorite drink at the bar?"

"I doubt that, in a cowboy bar," he said. "No, the walls are all wooden and covered with brands."

"All bars have neon signs and mirrors spouting brands of booze they sell. I don't remember any brand logo that looked like this," Amy said, pointing at the urn.

Jerry shook his head. "No, brands like in branding cattle. You know, those big hot iron bars with artwork at the end that they burn onto...well, you get the picture. Only on the walls inside the bar. They're covered with brands from various ranches throughout the county. Burned right into the wood. You can almost smell the smoke."

"And you just so happened to see a burn mark on the wall of a bar in Oakdale that matches our urn embossing?"

"I think so." Jerry scratched the side of his face, leaving a trail of dirt across his cheek. "I mean, it was only a week ago and I'm ..."

"A week ago? When did you go to a bar a week ago?" Amy interrupted.

"Uh, Mario and I went on that bike ride from Knights Ferry to Oakdale down Orange Blossom Road last week, remember?"

"Yeah, I remember. While I volunteered as an official on the 5K run for diabetes, you and Mario drove to the top of a hill, coasted down and called it exercise. Now I find out you guys wound up in a cowboy bar plowing down beers."

"They sell sodas, too," Jerry shot back.

"Did you have a soda?"

He turned his head and glanced around the trailer, avoiding eye contact. "They have a brand on the wall that looks like this embossing."

"Why don't you go in and call the Sheriff's Department? I don't think there's anything else here of interest, but I'll keep at it until you come back."

"OK." Jerry moved toward the trailer's door. "Remember, if you find something, let me see."

Amy looked under the cushions of the settee and saw a water storage tank. Its aluminum was cool to the touch in the hot trailer. She glanced back at the front and wondered if there was anything under the mattress that Jerry might have overlooked. She ducked and crab-walked to the back of the trailer to avoid hitting her head. She pulled the quilt off the floor, then folded it and stuck it out of the way.

Amy thought how great it would be to find a diamond ring or maybe a gold nugget. That would buy a dining room set or maybe a bathroom remodel.

The bed was in a solid wooden frame. Two small sheets of plywood atop the frame supported the mattress, leaving a storage cavity below. The thin mattress was covered in sheets that had been white but now were yellow with age.

Amy picked up a pillow and reached into the case to see if anything was hidden inside before tossing it to the floor. She scooted the mattress off of the frame and placed it on the floor, then climbed on top to access under the bed. She lifted one plywood panel off and peered into the half chamber below.

It was dark inside and hard to see but something sparkled in the dim light coming in from the window. Payday? she wondered, yet the thought of putting her hand into the dark space sent a chill up her spine. Amy hurried out of the trailer and into the garage to get a flashlight.

Back inside the trailer, she turned on the light and looked toward whatever was shining down there. It was just the glass surround from an old lantern. There were small shovels, jacks and tools laid neatly under the bed and Amy spied a coil of rope and carabiners tucked into a corner. The operation manual for the stove sat atop a small wooden box.

She pulled the box out and flipped it open, hoping to find something worthwhile. Old socket wrenches and sockets, a few screwdrivers and some Allen wrenches were inside. I don't know why I expected to find treasure all of a sudden, she thought. I didn't even want Jerry to bring this home. A twinge of guilt hit as she realized she was feeling greedy.

Amy went to put the wooden box back under the bed when she saw a small leather-bound book, a leather cord holding the covers closed. She picked it up and set it to the side while she replaced the box.

Amy replaced the half sheet of plywood on the frame and removed the sheet from the other side. The flashlight showed light bulbs, fuses, a canteen, a rolled-up tent or canopy and tent stakes and cord. She pressed on the fabric but didn't feel anything inside.

She replaced that piece of plywood and focused on the book. The dark tan leather felt dry and the cover was cracked from age. Amy could make out three barely visible letters etched in gold on the cover: Di___y.

She pulled on the cord that held it closed but it broke in her hand. Amy opened the book.

"The police will be here in about 15," Jerry's voice sounded suddenly behind her. "Did you find anything else?"

Amy recoiled, then quickly shut the book and held it against her.

"No, just some old tools and stuff. I'll put all this back in place. Why don't you take the urn and set it in the garage?"

"Will do."

The trailer bounced as Jerry climbed in and grabbed the urn. Amy set the book to the side and quickly replaced the mattress, then opened to a page at random. She saw a date and writing in flowing script. A woman's hand for sure, she thought, but as she touched the edges of the pages, they disintegrated. She closed the book before there was any more damage, thinking, someone's journal or diary.

Amy hid the book between two of the Sunset issues and climbed out of the trailer.

Jerry set up a table next to the little teardrop and started sorting what they'd already thrown out. Amy walked toward the house.

"What you got there?" he asked.

"A couple old Sunset magazines. I saw some recipes that looked good. I doubt the sheriff needs them."

"I jumped the gun throwing all this stuff out," Jerry said. "Maybe they need to see some of this stuff."

* * *

"When you said you found a body in a trailer, I mean, you could have explained the body was ashes, Mr. Curtis," Deputy Radcliff said. He held a clipboard and jotted notes as he glanced around the dilapidated trailer. Radcliff was 6 feet tall, sported tree trunks for arms, and his uniform shirt was a size too small and showed off his physique. His hair was short and spiked with gel. The handcuffs, gun, baton and other items on his utility belt jingled when he moved. "I didn't need to get here this quick."

"If your dispatcher had given me some time, I would have," Jerry said.

"You say you found the ashes in this trailer?"

"Yes."

"And you bought this trailer from who?" Radcliff asked.

"We found it and brought it home."

"And where did you find it?" The deputy's eyes widened as he waited for an answer.

"Out at Tuolumne River Regional Park, buried in the brush next to the river," Jerry said, glancing at the trailer's flattened tires and the vegetation lodged underneath it.

"You know," Radcliff said, "you should have reported this to the Modesto Police Department, since it's a vehicle and all and it's their jurisdiction. Still, I'll make a judgment and figure that perhaps the value of this isn't worth the MPD's time." He stared at the tires' cracked sidewalls and algae patina.

"Now, back to the urn," Radcliff continued. "You assume it has someone's ashes in it?"

"It says 'CB Memorial Home,' " Jerry said. "I mean, it's printed in ink on the bottom. And look, it's got these embossed letters in the wax seal at the top. I think I've seen that same logo on the wall at the H Bar B in Oakdale."

"Do much drinking, do you, Mr. Curtis?"

"No. I've hardly ever ... wait a minute. I'm just trying to help. Amy, tell him," Jerry urged.

"He doesn't do much drinking, officer," she said, turning toward her husband, lips pursed and shaking her head. "Based on what we've seen in this trailer, it appears that nobody's been inside since 1997. What if a relative of the deceased has been searching for the ashes?" Amy asked.

"Well..."

"What if it was one of your relatives, officer?" she interrupted.

"If it was my loony Aunt Mabel, I never would have said a word," Radcliff replied. "But, I understand your concern. I'll take the ashes back to the coroner's office," he said. "Try not to disturb too much in the trailer for the next week or so. The coroner might want to take a look at where this was found." He looked at the urn.

Amy and Jerry nodded.

"Here's my card," Radcliff said. "If you find anything that you think might help with the identification of the remains, give me a call."

* * *

Jerry followed Amy into the house. She sat at the kitchen counter and tapped on the Sunset magazines, motioning him into the chair next to her.

"That cop was kinda pushy, huh?" Jerry said.

"Not to me," Amy answered. "You need to present an air of authority. They'll get the message."

"Last time I tried to do that, the cop decided a speeding ticket wasn't enough and that my tires were a tad too worn. Cost me a bunch to be authoritative," Jerry said.

"Maybe it's a woman thing. You're lucky you have one of the best on your side."

"I'm so glad I married you," Jerry said, leaning over to kiss her cheek.

"I didn't show you this earlier," Amy said as she lifted the magazines off the book. "But I think this is the diary of someone who maybe owned that little trailer."

CHAPTER THREE
Louise Kantro

"A diary?"

"You look surprised," Amy said, undoing the band of her ponytail and fluffing her hair.

"I guess I expected camping stuff. I can see taking books on a camping trip – I mean for a person who likes to read. I didn't realize there would be anything really personal in the trailer, and now we've got two things, ashes and a diary."

Amy nodded. What had seemed like such an adventure was becoming a kind of responsibility.

"I guess we really do need to figure out who these people are."

"Even if they want their trailer back," Jerry added.

"Hey, um, honey bun? It's fine if you stop for a beer with the guys sometimes. I shouldn't have given you a hard time about it."

He smiled.

"I know you don't overdo." Amy gathered up

her hair to start a new ponytail.

"You know," she said, "I found myself getting greedy when we were looking through the trailer, and I don't like that side of myself. I was hoping we'd find some jewelry or – oh, I don't know – money?"

"Yeah," Jerry said. "Me, too. I didn't even think about jewelry but I got caught up in the idea of getting something big for free. I'd love to have the trailer for camping, especially when ..."

He gave her a little smile, and she knew he meant "when we have kids."

She was the one who had set up their save-for-a-baby plan, and they were almost, but not quite, ready to start trying. Jerry knew how worried Amy was that they might get tangled up in the problems that some couples in their 30s faced these days. Sure, there were plenty of women who had babies in their 40s but her friend Susanna from work had been experiencing some difficulties and said her doctor told her it was harder for women over 30 and men over 35 to conceive. Maybe it had something to do with the foods we eat or our environment, Susanna had speculated, shrugging.

Amy wondered whether she and Jerry would end up going to a fertility clinic. Maybe they would decide to adopt. One way or the other, she was determined to have a family.

She brought herself back to the moment.

"The thing is," Jerry said, "it's not just the possibility of getting the trailer. It's that the people who owned this trailer are real people."

"I'm curious about them, too," Amy said. "I wonder how old they were, how long they'd been together. Maybe it wasn't even a couple but I figure there was a woman in the equation if there's a diary involved. Is that sexist?"

"Men don't write in diaries," Jerry said decisively. "I'm going to take a shower."

"OK. I think I'll start looking through the diary," Amy said.

She settled at the kitchen table and held the diary for a minute, looking it over. When she opened it, some dirt fell onto the table. Some of the pages looked as if they'd been gnawed on by animals. The only explanation Amy could come up with was that the diary might have been thrown away, maybe just outside the trailer, since it was clean dirt, not the stinky stuff that would have come from a trashcan or dumpster. This led to a whole new thought. Maybe the diary was someone else's – something the trailer owners had found. For some reason, Amy was convinced that Ms. Trailer Owner was the diarist. Maybe Ms. T.O. regretted throwing it away and later retrieved it. The fact that it had been wrapped in a quilt might mean that she had been keeping it hidden. Had Mr. T.O. known about the diary? Had he respected Ms. T.O.'s privacy enough not to read it?

Darn. Amy hadn't thought about how she was about to violate the writer's privacy. A diary is supposed to be a safe place for secrets.

She took a deep breath; she wanted to read it. It was probably mostly boring stuff, which was one reason she never had been driven to keep a diary.

Today I went to work and stopped at the store on the way home. Blah-blah-blah.

Amy reminded herself that the reason she wanted to look through the diary was to see if it would lead to the owner of the trailer. And really, after 17 years, what might have seemed like really personal, private stuff probably had been resolved long ago or the person had just moved on. If there were earth-shattering secrets inside, she would tell Jerry it was too personal, try to forget what she'd read, and put the book aside.

Yeah, right.

The first thing to do was not exactly flip through it, considering its condition, but turn the pages carefully just to see if any names, addresses or phone numbers were recorded.

But when Amy opened to the first page, she saw that the writing was not going to be easy to decipher. Almost every page had torn or smudged spots and what she could see she couldn't necessarily read. On Page 2, she was able to make out a passage about going to dinner at someone's house and how Ms. T.O. hated seafood. Apparently someone had gotten drunk and done something rude – here Amy encountered some smudges – that caused Ms. T.O. to consider turning down future invitations to Doug and Mar—'s parties.

Mary? Marie? Margie? Marta? Marguerite? This was going to take a while.

She was surprised that she hadn't thought of it before, but Mr. and Ms. T.O. could be dead. That would make looking through the diary less intrusive, but it would be sad. Amy didn't want them to be dead, though she and Jerry wanted their trailer. This was turning out to be both a puzzle and surprisingly emotional.

"Jerry?" she called as she walked toward the closed bathroom door in the master bedroom.

"Do you think the people who owned the trailer are OK? I mean, do you think they're still alive?"

Jerry flung open the door, a towel wrapped around his waist. He walked toward the bed, where he had laid out clean clothes.

"That's the first thing I wondered about," he said, "but I don't know why. I mean, why is it any more likely that they're dead than alive?"

"It must be the urn. It made us think about death."

Nodding, Jerry stopped rubbing his hair dry and pulled a T-shirt over his head.

"I'm really into this diary thing right now," Amy said. "I want to get Tracy over tomorrow to help me. It's hard to read the handwriting, and since Tracy is a teacher, I figure she can read anything."

"Works for me," Jerry said. "They're barbecuing for her family today, so why don't we provide dinner? I'll make my famous chili. Mario and I have some business to conduct, anyway. I want to throw a few bucks his way for the tow."

"He'll probably say no, but it's worth a try," Amy said.

Mario and Tracy had been living pretty frugally since they'd had Bianca, which was one of several reasons Amy had planned to save fifty percent of her take-home pay for at least two years before they started trying to have a baby. Now they had just a few more months to go. The only reason it had been possible to save that much was that when the housing market bottomed out, they bought an older house for cheap. Jerry was fixing up the house a little at a time, with some help from Mario. What they saved monthly with a low house payment and the tax deduction was helping. Amy, who had grown up in west Modesto, worn thrift-store clothes and taken the bus everywhere, wanted the cushion of an entire year's pay, especially since lots of people were losing their jobs or getting their hours cut. When she became a mother, Amy would be OK with part-time hours if they had a cushion. She was willing to take it on faith that Jerry's twelve years at the hospital meant that he probably would be able to hang on to his job.

"Amy?"

"Uh?"

"You OK?"

"Yeah. I was into one of my baby daydreams," she said sheepishly. Everywhere she went these days she saw pregnant women, babies, and toddlers.

"I'll call Mario," Jerry said. "And then, how about we get takeout from Enrique's?"

Before the diet, they'd usually gotten takeout on Saturday nights. Now, after more than six months on a strict diet, Amy was craving something gooey and cheesy. She would make a big salad for tomorrow.

No, she should stick with the diet. She'd really trimmed down and didn't want to slip back, especially since she might be pregnant by Christmas.

"It'll go straight to my hips," Amy said.

"More of you to love," Jerry answered.

She stuck out her tongue at him.

"Aren't you on maintenance now?"

She nodded. What good was being on maintenance if you couldn't splurge once in a while? "Let's watch a movie," she said. "You get the food. I'll find the movie."

"Not a chick flick," Jerry said. That was always his only requirement.

* * *

Bianca sat in the corner of the kitchen on the floor. She had lined up several dolls and stuffed animals and was pretending to feed them. With her dark brown hair in long, tight braids, only the shape of her face resembled Tracy, who was a blue-eyed strawberry blonde.

"How do you fit all those critters in your bag?" Amy asked.

"It's not easy," Tracy said. "Since the menagerie can occupy her for a long time, I don't leave home without them."

"Let's get started then," Amy said, knowing that "a long time" with a 3-year-old was not all that long.

Amy had all the supplies on the table, including the diary, a magnifying glass, a notebook, a flashlight, and two pencils. She had assigned herself the job of note taker. Tracy was in charge of reading aloud what was in the diary, with Amy helping if she couldn't decipher a word or phrase.

After the first page, Amy congratulated herself that she'd been right about Tracy's "teacher" eyes. If Tracy couldn't read it, neither could Amy.

For the first five pages, Amy took a lot of notes. After a while, she drew a line on the notebook page and wrote "just summarizing unless noted otherwise." If she did quote from the diary, she used quotation marks.

Twenty minutes later, they were about one-fourth of the way through when Bianca's chatter with her dolls and animals stopped. Leaving them sprawled willy-nilly on the floor, she raced over to Tracy and hugged her legs. Tracy called it "checking in."

"Want to see what we're doing?" Amy asked, holding out her arms. Bianca came over and, without saying a word, allowed herself to be lifted onto Amy's lap. "No, you can't touch it because it's so old, but look at the cover. It's kind of pretty."

"Where's Daddy?" Bianca asked, shimmying out

of Amy's lap. Her Mary Jane shoes clunked as they hit the floor.

Bianca was now operating on "short attention span."

"In the garage," Tracy said. "Pick up your friends first."

When the last stuffed animal had been shoved into the bag, Tracy took Bianca to the garage door.

"I'll see what the guys are doing," she said. "Power tools and curious children are not a good combination."

"Mario? Jer? Can Bianca come see what you're up to?"

"Sure," Jerry said. "We're just sitting here shooting the breeze."

"This might give us another 20 minutes," Tracy said when she got back to the kitchen table. "Then maybe she'll be ready for a nap. Obviously, going through this diary is going to take a while."

"I think Jerry's got some big camping plans for us – all of us – if we get to keep the trailer," Amy said.

"Five people are not gonna fit in that trailer."

"True," Amy said, "but that doesn't mean you guys can't use it."

"Not sure I'd like camping," Tracy said, "but it would be worth trying at least once."

"OK, back to work," her friend said. "After work and nap, we'll stuff our bellies."

* * *

The next day, on the way home from her job in Ceres, Amy turned right on I Street, as she did every day so she could drive under the "Water, Wealth, Contentment, Health" arch and past the Gallo Performing Arts Center, with its elegant facade. Her mother had been in plays in high school and had taken Amy and her brother to local productions. She had died 10 years before Gallo was built, but Amy thought of her every time she drove past it. Turning left at 14th and then right onto J, she drove past the statue of the teens from George Lucas' American Graffiti. It marked the start of the J Street "drag," where kids had shown off their cars, trying to impress each other.

Her mind drifted back to the diary.

Absently cranking up the air conditioner, Amy wondered if the trailer's owners had spent weekend nights on McHenry Avenue when they were young. Since time had stopped for the trailer in 1997, if the couple had been in their 20s or 30s, they would have been in high school in the 1970s or 1980s. Maybe they were even older. Maybe they had known George Lucas.

Ms. T.O. was not a teenager. There were no little hearts and doodles, very little slang, though there were abbreviations. There were no gushy-crushy entries about cute guys or agonized comments about snotty girls who had gotten on the diary-writer's bad side. Most of the daily stuff had to do with the kind of life a grown woman lives: errands, little problems at work (Tracy had offered up the possibility that she might have worked at a school, maybe as a secretary), some exploration of the kind of social life in which people sometimes partied a little hard, and a relationship that seemed to be generally satisfactory. A bit dull but also kind of sweet.

It was the entries on the last few pages of the diary that had stopped Amy and Tracy short. Unfortunately, they had been heavily smudged, so the sentences were fractured, requiring guesswork.

Something sad had happened to, or somehow involved, a baby. It could have been the trailer owners' baby. It could have been an unborn baby. A miscarriage? Maybe it was the baby of a friend or family member. There simply wasn't enough readable information for them to figure it out.

They had decided immediately that the urn didn't hold the ashes of a baby. It was too heavy and there was nothing in its design to indicate that the loved one had been an infant. Also, they believed, though they both knew that this was purely emotional, that most parents would bury an infant.

Amy had thought about this baby all day long at work, careful to double-check so she wouldn't make mistakes. A couple of her co-workers in the medical billing office had asked if she was OK, so she must have looked worried. Now, as she stopped at red lights, turned corners and tried to block out the late afternoon sun that was peeking around her visor, Amy reconstructed what she and Tracy had pieced together. She couldn't quite remember what words had led her to worry about this baby. She would have to review her notes and see if Jerry wanted to put some time into putting the puzzle pieces together.

Yesterday she had said to Tracy, "Let's not tell the guys about the baby – at least not yet."

Tracy had nodded, obviously getting into the "we're detectives" thing.

The only thing Jerry had asked was, "Did you girls have a good time with that diary?" a comment Amy thought was a little dismissive.

Still, marriage was about sharing, and she wanted to know what Jerry thought. Sometimes he had a way of cutting to the chase on things she had managed to complicate.

Of course, she would have to feed him first. He had cooked the chili yesterday, so it was her turn to make dinner and Jerry came home from his hospital maintenance job tired and hungry.

After dinner, she would approach him about the diary and, specifically, about the baby. If he wasn't interested or thought she was doing her baby-obsession thing, she would take on this line of investigation by herself. She knew Tracy would help if she could, though her job and Bianca kept her pretty busy.

She wondered if Jerry had been thinking about their find – well, his find – all day at work the way she had been.

CHAPTER FOUR
R. Garrett Wilson

Jerry had taken the country roads home from Turlock instead of the freeway, something he often did after a rough day. He had been having plenty of those ever since Emanuel Medical Center opened its new cancer center. The expansions at the hospital had been happening so fast that they outpaced the maintenance personnel, which meant that Jerry and his crew had been putting in a lot of overtime. He didn't look forward to the conversation tonight when he would tell Amy about having to work Saturday – his third Saturday in four weeks. He didn't look forward to telling her why the seat of his car was soaking wet, either.

He pulled onto his street and noticed Andreas at the community mailbox. Andreas, a 68-year-old Greek who had lived in the United States since he was 3, waved. Jerry waved back and then hit the button on the garage door remote. When he pulled into the driveway, he could see Amy's car and the teardrop – he would have to park in the driveway today. He clubbed the steering wheel and grabbed his tools.

As he was getting out of the car, he heard Andreas' flip-flops. Jerry didn't have to turn around to picture Andreas' shuffle, the pseudo-run he did when trying to catch up to people.

"Jer. Jer?"

Jerry wished he had stopped at the store to buy milk or ice cream, but he didn't have an excuse to cut off the conversation today. He sighed, put on a smile and turned to face his neighbor. "Hi, Andreas."

"Jer, I'm so happy to see you. Rose and I saw the police the other day and thought for sure you were being arrested. It's always the quiet ones."

"Sheriff's deputy. And I'm not that quiet."

Andreas raised his eyebrows.

The only person Jerry knew who liked to talk more than Andreas was Andreas' wife, Rosalie. By comparison, Jerry was the quiet neighbor, but so was everyone else in the world. "Tell Rose I'm just fine. We found that trailer near the river a few days back and needed a coroner —"

"You found a body? Ahhh..." Andreas' hand went to his mouth, touching the grey stubble of his short beard.

"No, not a body, just an urn."

"And you kept the trailer? Have you seen any ghosts coming out of it?"

"No."

"Out of paintings in your house?"

"No."

"Any portals to heaven, hell or other worlds?"

"Andreas, come on. I've had a long day."

"If you need a paranormal investigator, I'm your man."

"Was that before or after you were a Navy SEAL?"

"Um, let's see. I was at the Gaslight Theater when I was a paranormal investigator, but —"

"Great, it wasn't even a recent part."

Andreas had acted in various groups that worked out of the Gaslight Theater in Denair early in his career before he'd joined traveling guilds. A few years before he retired, he'd been accepted into the Townsend Opera Players in Modesto, back in the same area from which he'd started. Jerry had thought Andreas wanted to be here because of family ties, but in the two years they had been neighbors, he never had seen Andreas go anywhere or anyone come visit him.

"I did a lot of research for that. I could practically do the job. No respect for my dedication."

Jerry didn't say that he thought paranormal investigators were actors to begin with. He knew that would open a whole new line of discussion. "Look, I'm wet; I'm tired; I really want to get cleaned up."

"Did you find out who it is, was, whatever? I bet there were a lot of clues inside."

Jerry sighed and put down his tools. Come on Amy, come save me, he thought. "No, we haven't figured anything out."

Andreas took a few steps toward the garage, and Jerry regretted setting down his tools. It wasn't an invite.

"Are you keeping the trailer?"

"I think so," Jerry replied. There was a slight pause, with Andreas staring at him as if he were waiting for more details. "We're trying to."

"You should really find out who owns it – and who's in the urn."

"We've been trying," Jerry said. "The trailer has no license plate, no VIN —"

"Well, it wouldn't have that, would it?"

"Why not?"

"It's a kit. Pretty sure." Andreas walked into the garage and scoped out the teardrop. "Definitely a kit. Probably late '40s, but they made this kit through the '60s, I think."

"How do you know?"

"Oh, I used to go to gatherings, at least the local ones. I went to one near Año Nuevo as well, so I guess it wasn't only local ones, but mostly around here. Actually, Año Nuevo is pretty close. Been there? They have elephant seals."

"Gatherings?"

"Yeah, there used to be pretty big teardrop clubs all over the U.S., probably other places, too. Every now and then there would be a big campout, and they called it a gathering. Rose and I had a teardrop back in the '90s, well, we shared it with a couple of other Opera

Players, and we went to a few of them, the gatherings. Let's see, there was a pretty big one at Don Pedro Reservoir and an under-advertised one at Turlock Lake. And the..."

Andreas was counting the events on his fingers when Jerry held his hand up. He went back to describing the gatherings instead of naming them. "Sometimes it would only be one or two clubs going, but more often it was open to everyone. I don't know what happened to the one at Turlock Lake, but it was a disappointment after the Don Pedro gathering. I mean it was as if..." Andreas stopped midsentence, this time of his own accord, and nodded toward the house.

Jerry turned to see the door from the garage to the laundry room open and Amy standing there. She looked good, hair done and makeup freshly applied. "Jer, dinner's ready."

"OK, hon. I'll be there in a few minutes."

"It's hot now."

The aroma of teriyaki sauce and rice hit him and made his stomach growl. "Just give me a few minutes."

Amy looked at both of them before going back inside. Jerry would have to explain later. He was surprised his neighbor had real, not acting, experience with something Jerry was trying to investigate. He knew Amy would be, too.

"Oh, I shouldn't keep you," Andreas said. "You know what they say about women and a hot meal? Well, it was Ford who said it: 'Tell the truth, work hard and come to dinner on time.' I'm not really sure it was about women, come to think of it, but it makes the most sense to —"

"No, it's not a problem." Great, Jerry thought, the one time I'm interested and now he's willing to go home, and Amy's made something nice. "Tell me more about the teardrop clubs."

"Not much to tell. They're all over the place. or at least they were. A whole bunch of people with similar vehicles sharing about exciting things they've discovered and work-arounds to common problems – just like the PT Cruiser club Modesto used to have or the RV clubs. What was the name of the PT club? Highway 99 PT, or something like that?"

Jerry shrugged. "And someone in one of these clubs would be able to tell me who owned this trailer?"

"If the owners were part of a club, maybe. I know that's a kit and there were lots of people with kits, so it would all come down to the year of the kit and customizations on the inside."

"We had an urn inside – that should narrow it down."

"You mean, they had an urn inside."

"Yeah."

"I doubt that would be well known to club members. However, people who did customizations were always showing those off. The Golden Generation guys were always doing stuff," Andreas said.

"Customizations?"

"Yeah, like storage solutions. Storage was always

a big talking point since there wasn't much of any in the trailer."

There was a pause in the conversation, a true pause. It felt strange. Andreas knelt down to examine the hitch, tires and fenders. Jerry moved next to him, trying to figure out what he was thinking.

Andreas pointed at a rubber-lined plastic cap in the side of the trailer. "See this, here? This isn't standard, not on the models I saw. If you take the cap out, you might fit a phone line or coax cable. It isn't big enough for an electrical plug. Right now it is capped to be watertight. This is the stuff the clubs will notice right off."

Jerry nodded.

"Some of this is still in good condition," Andreas said, motioning to the door and siding. "But you'll have to hammer out the fenders, get new tires and replace the hitch coupler."

Jerry was making mental notes of things to fix. However, this isn't where he wanted the conversation to move. He stood and asked, "How would I find a club?"

"Back in the day, you would look in a magazine or talk to someone at the dealership. I learned about mine from a lady at Knights Ferry. You know, where the covered bridge is. Well, anyway, we had gone on a white-water rafting trip and we met her on the boat. Nice lady. She told me about her club and gave me her contact info."

"You still have it?"

"The contact info? No, that was over 15 years ago. I don't camp anymore, much less raft. Why don't you try using the Internet? They have everything on there these days. I bet you could find a club that way."

"Thanks, Andreas," Jerry said, sticking out his hand.

Andreas took his hand and replied, "Not a problem." Then, as if looking at Jerry for the first time, he asked, "Why are you all wet?"

"There was water coming out of the lighting fixtures in the women's bathroom," he said. Andreas started to say something, but Jerry cut him off. "It's a long story and I really do have to shower and eat."

Andreas smiled and nodded. "Glad you weren't arrested, although that would have made a great story. Are you documenting everything you are doing? You know, if the person in that urn is famous, like Jimmy Hoffa, you can make millions selling your story. I would —"

"Dinner's getting cold," Amy said from the door. "I love you, honey."

Andreas waved at her. Jerry grabbed his tools from the driveway and started heading for the door when he heard Andreas shuffle away. Found someone else. He was smiling and shaking his head as he entered the house.

Amy was sitting at the kitchen bar, facing him. Dinner was on a warming plate and the place settings were out.

Something's up, Jerry thought. He tried

to remember if this was a special day. "It smells wonderful."

She smiled at him. "So what was that about?"

"Oh, he used to have a teardrop, knows a lot about them."

"In reality, or an acting job?"

"In reality. And he told me about —" Jerry's phone rang, stopping him midsentence. He held it up, looked at the number, and his shoulders dropped. "Gatherings," he finished before answering. "Yeah ... yeah ... I could, but I really want to change first ... Yeah, I'm still wet ... How long? ... 'K. Bye."

Amy's demeanor changed. She looked tired.

"I gotta go," Jerry said. He looked at Amy and around the kitchen, then scowled at the floor. Had he taken the freeway home instead of the back roads, or had he come into the house instead of talking to Andreas, he would have had time to eat with his wife. He didn't know how to tell her that she deserved better, that he wanted to spend time with her, so he took off his shirt and simply said, "Randy's sick. I have the first half of his shift."

She smiled sympathetically and said, "I'll pack dinner for you."

"Oh, I also have to work Saturday."

As he headed down the hall to get a new shirt, he heard Amy packing up his dinner in the kitchen, much louder than normal. He knew he was going to have to be ready to do something special on Sunday.

ASHES
IN A
TEARDROP

CHAPTER FIVE

Jennie Bass

Amy sighed as she watched her husband's car back out of the driveway. Getting angry with Jerry would serve no purpose. "Stupid Randy," she muttered under her breath, feeling slightly guilty for her uncharitable thoughts as she wiped down the counter. It wasn't his fault either, but there was no one here to judge her.

She took her frustrations out on the kitchen and found that in her snit, she worked much more efficiently than usual. Still, she was in a bad mood and had more time on her hands than desired. She was too wound up for TV, and any thought of the diary held no appeal. Amy wanted to improve her frame of mind, and the tragedy hinted at within its pages certainly wouldn't accomplish that. Besides, staring at it wouldn't make the broken sentences and smudged words legible enough to finish their sad tale.

Amy wandered into the living room, thinking of the diary with a flash of clarity. It had been deliberately concealed, she decided. Why else would it have been in such an inconvenient location? But who had hidden it? Ms. T.O. seemed to have been in a healthy relationship that would require no such deceit, so it didn't seem like it could have been her. Although maybe she had put it there in an attempt to hide the unhappy memories housed between its pages.

Reading the diary had placed Amy in the shoes of a woman who had lost a baby. Although the decipherable details were sketchy on whether the child belonged to Ms. T.O., somehow Amy thought it had. Several questions had been dancing through her head since the discovery of the yellowed pages beneath the bed, but they were taking on an uncomfortable urgency. Who was the woman who had unintentionally let Amy into her life? Why were there ashes in a teardrop trailer, of all places? Were they her remains? Was she even connected to the urn?

With a new resolve, Amy retrieved her cell from her purse and called the third number on speed dial.

"Hey Tracy, how would you like to help me ditch my diet tonight and go out for a couple of drinks? I know it's late notice ... You're in your pajamas already? Oh come on, we're not that old yet! Let's be a little spontaneous while we still can!" She listened for a moment. "No, nothing's wrong. Yes, he got called into work tonight ... No, Jerry and I aren't fighting about his overtime." She let out a huff of exasperation. "Oh, for crying out loud, are you going to go or not?

Great! I'll pick you up in half an hour. An hour? We're both married. No one's going to look at us anyway, why waste all that time?" she sighed. "Fine, an hour, but you'd better be ready when I get there."

* * *

"The H B?" Tracy asked skeptically as Amy searched for parking.

"It appears to be a popular place."

"The H B???" Tracy repeated.

"It's not the 'H B,'" Amy said, showing off her newly acquired knowledge, courtesy of Jerry. "You pronounce the 'bar.' Get it? It's a bar, the 'H - Bar - B.'"

Tracy looked unimpressed and Amy shrugged. "Maybe you have to be from Oakdale to appreciate it."

Its simple brick exterior could have been there from the town's early days. It sported only a few upgrades, including a neon sign stating the bar's name in bright orange. The watering hole was in the middle of Oakdale on a corner of Highway 108 where the limited parking could spill onto a side street.

"Doesn't look like much," Tracy said.

"It's supposed to be an authentic cowboy bar," Amy said.

"Where are the horses?"

"There's one right there," Amy smirked as she gestured across the street to a life-size metal statue of a man riding a bucking horse. "Just go inside and try to have some fun!" she admonished her friend.

"Fine, but when you asked if I wanted to go out, I envisioned more of a ladies' night. You know, margaritas, karaoke, a late call for a ride home since neither one of us could drive?"

Amy opened the door to the sound of an angry woman crooning about her plans for vengeance against a background of drums and steel guitars. She peered doubtfully into the dim interior. "I don't think we'll find karaoke here, but I'm pretty sure you can find margaritas. We'll see what we can do about needing a ride home later, OK?"

Tracy snorted and followed her friend into the building.

"Oh my," Amy said.

"No kidding," Tracy agreed. Every wall held multiple trophies, the kind that used to breathe.

"This reminds me of a horror movie, one where all the animals come to life and take their revenge on the hunters," Amy said out of the corner of her mouth.

Tracy snickered. "Holy crap, I can't believe this place is here. It's like stepping through a portal from California straight to Texas! Where are all these cowboys from?"

"Presumably from Oakdale," Amy answered dryly. "This is 'The Cowboy Capital of the World.'"

Tracy's observation was valid, Amy thought as they made their way to the bar. Not everyone was wearing cowboy boots and Stetsons, but at least half were. All the seats were taken, so the women stood behind those fortunate enough to have secured a stool. Waiting patiently for the bartender's attention, they continued to take in the scene, avoiding the glassy gaze of anything hanging from the wall.

Amy caught the eye of an older gentleman dressed in jeans and a T-shirt. Her gaze dropped involuntarily to his feet, which were tucked beneath his bar stool. Ah, he had boots on. "You're one of the lucky ones," she commented with a smile, gesturing at his stool.

"You've got to either get here early or have the luck of the Irish to get a seat at the bar here," the man responded with a grin. "Fortunately, I have both. I'd offer you my seat, but as there are two of you, I'm not sure how helpful that would be."

"Oh, don't worry about it. We're more interested in taking in the sights anyway."

"We are?" Tracy chimed in.

"Yes, we are," Amy answered with a pointed look at her friend.

"Oh right, yes we are!" Tracy said, suddenly recalling the reason behind their visit. "Do you remember a brand around here with double Rs?"

"Not off the top of my head," the man said slowly, "but I've been coming here for so long that I rarely notice the decor anymore. Why do you ask?"

"Oh, we're just curious," Amy said with a nonchalance she didn't feel. She shot an annoyed look at her friend, silently chastising her for the less-than-subtle approach. "I saw the brand somewhere recently and my husband thought he remembered it from here."

"OK. Well, let's see what we can find."

"Oh no, thank you for the offer, but we don't want to disturb you."

"Sure we do," Tracy interrupted with a wink. "If he's a regular, he can probably find it faster than we can, and then we can relax and have our margaritas. My name's Tracy, by the way, and this crazy lady is my friend Amy."

"Pleased to meet you, ladies. I'm Chuck," he said, offering his hand. "Let's get you started on those margaritas while we look."

"That's what I'm talking about," Tracy said. "You only get so many nights out once you have kids — why squander a perfectly good one?"

"You didn't even want to come out tonight!" Amy protested indignantly.

"What can I say? You're very persuasive."

At a gesture from Chuck, the bartender, also in jeans and a T-shirt, approached. "Just in case you don't know, we only take cash here," she said with a smile after taking their orders.

"Thanks for the warning," Amy answered. She turned to Tracy once the bartender had gone and said, "Driving home won't be a problem. I only have around 20 bucks on me!"

"Me, too!"

It was suddenly quiet as the song ended. Amy expected the twang of country to take its place and was surprised to hear Guns N' Roses instead. "Quite an eclectic selection of music," she observed to no one in particular.

"It fits us," Chuck said with a shrug.

"I can see that," Amy said, looking around. The bar was full of people in plaid and boots, T-shirts and tennis shoes, but some sported suits and loafers, dresses and heels. They all appeared to be having fun.

Their drinks arrived, and Tracy took a sip. "Excellent," she said to the bartender. The woman, in her 30s and clearly in charge, smiled as if to say, "Of course it is. I made it."

"All right," Chuck said, slapping the bar and rising from his stool. "Let's go find this brand."

"I doubt my husband would have made it too far from the bar, but I haven't seen anything yet. What about by the restroom?" Axl Rose's caterwauling in the background gave Amy an idea. "Or the jukebox?" Unfortunately, neither area had the brand, and as the bar got more crowded, it became increasingly difficult to examine the walls. It wasn't until Amy and Tracy were nursing their second drinks that Chuck finally found the brand near the exit.

"That's it!" Amy cried out in excitement as they stared at the wall. She was impressed that Jerry had noticed, much less remembered it. The brand was nearly hidden by a diner who seemed unnerved by their stares.

"Great," Tracy said. "We've seen it. What

now?"

"Oh. That's a good question. Um, Chuck, do you have any idea where we might find the origin of this brand?"

"Well, you could ask the owner of the bar, or maybe some old timers."

Amy and Tracy switched their attention from the brand to him, to the apparent relief of the diner and his companion.

"Yes," Chuck said, his blue eyes twinkling, "there are occasionally people here who surpass me in age."

"Of course there are," Amy assured him. "You're only, what, in your 50s?"

Chuck snorted. "I was in my 50s a decade ago, and I look like it. That brand isn't one I'm familiar with, but I'm not a rancher. Let's see if we can find someone who is."

Unfortunately, the owner of the bar was out, according to the bartender, the ranchers all had gone home. "They tend to keep early hours," she explained. "What's this about, anyway?"

"My husband and I found an urn with this symbol pressed into the wax," Amy said. "We're just trying to find who it belongs to."

"Huh. Is that the urn they found in a storage shed in Modesto?"

"No. According to the paper, they know who those ashes belong to, but they just can't find anyone who wants them."

"How sad is that?" Tracy asked.

"I know, right? Anyhow, the Sheriff's Department has the urn, but we thought we might be able to find out something on our own."

"Won't the coroner be able to identify the remains?" Chuck asked.

"Probably," Amy said, "but it's not like they're going to share that information with us."

The bartender looked at them for a moment. Amy could tell she wanted more information but was too good at her job to pry.

"Well, I'm sorry I couldn't help you. You want anything else to drink?" The trio declined, and she went to attend to other customers.

Chuck leaned against the bar. "So where did you find the urn?"

"In a trailer we found in the river," Amy said, then filled him in.

"I don't know if it'll do any good, but if you like, you can leave your number with me," he said. "If anyone recognizes the brand, I'll let you know."

"That would be really nice, but I don't want to put you out any more than I already have," Amy said.

"Don't mention it. All we do here is sit around shooting the breeze. This will give us something interesting to talk about for a change."

Amy smiled. "Well, thank you, Chuck. I really appreciate it."

* * *

An hour later, Amy thanked her friend as she dropped her off. "It was actually kind of fun," Tracy said as she got out of the car. "We just need to take more cash with us next time."

"Next time?" Amy teased.

"Sure, why not? The drinks were good, and I liked Chuck."

Amy waited until Tracy was inside before driving off. At home, she was greeted by an empty house instead of her husband, who should have been there. "Stupid Randy," she said as she crawled into bed. Despite her irritation, she drifted quickly into a sleep full of crying babies, dusty books, and restless figures wearing cowboy hats.

* * *

Amy's strategy for unwinding after work involved loud music and singing at the top of her lungs with the car windows rolled down. The following Monday it worked well, although it did make hearing her cell phone problematic. Fortunately, Jerry was used to having to call her multiple times before getting a response. He finally caught her during a lull between songs and got straight to the point.

"Amy, the strangest thing just happened. Some guy just called, saying that the trailer was his."

"Really? How on earth did he hear about it?"

"He said he read about it in a sheriff's report

and then got our number from them."

"Huh, so that deputy filed a report after all, even though he gave us grief for contacting them."

"Well no, he didn't, but I'll get to that in a minute. This guy, Bob, couldn't tell me anything specific about the trailer. He claimed it belonged to his uncle, but he certainly didn't mind throwing him under the bus, so to speak. Bob claims that his uncle was an alcoholic, got drunk one night, and through some mishap, the trailer rolled into the river."

"You're kidding!"

"Nope, although I'm pretty sure Bob is full of crap. I called Radcliff — the deputy who took the urn, remember? — to complain about them giving out our number. He denied it and assured me that no one else at the department had either. And here's the kicker: Radcliff never filed a report. He said it wasn't worth their resources."

"But what about the urn? Didn't he file a report on that?"

"He did, but only someone who was already looking for it would find it. It's not like they posted it on *Modbee* or something."

"So this guy knows about the trailer, but we don't know how. He didn't mention anything about the urn?"

"Not a word, and I didn't want to ask any leading questions."

"Right."

There was a lull in the conversation as both

of them chased down their thoughts. Amy spoke first. "OK, here's what I think. There's no law that says we have to hand over the trailer to any yahoo who says it's his. He should be able to show us proof, and if he can't, then we should keep it."

She continued, feeling the need to justify keeping something that wasn't really theirs. "This guy already lied about how he found out about the trailer, so he could be lying about owning it too. Hey, did he say why his uncle isn't claiming it?"

"No, he didn't. I just assumed he's dead, but even if he is, who's to say the nephew was the one who inherited his stuff?"

"Exactly, and what's more," Amy said, "I'm not sure I believe this story about Mr. T.O. being a drunk. That place was spotless; everything was neatly stored. That trailer was well taken care of, even loved, if Andreas is right about all of the upgrades. I don't think that trailer ended up in the river through any misdeeds of Mr. T.O. And another thing, there was no mention in the diary of problems with alcohol."

"Agreed," Jerry said, although he felt there were a few holes in her logic, the most glaring being her assumption that alcoholics didn't take care of their belongings. He also questioned the validity of relying on a diary that may or may not have belonged to the trailer's owners. However, valid reasons or not, his gut instinct was that "Bob," if indeed that was his name, had no right to the trailer.

CHAPTER SIX

Alexandra Deabler

The sun slipped into the room, forcing its way under the lids of a very tired Jerry. He clenched his eyes shut, protesting the inevitable announcement of morning. His effort was in vain, though. The bright beams were unrelenting. Jerry's eyes snapped open, bloodshot from a night of late work and bad sleep.

"Did you want coffee?" Jerry asked Amy with a yawn, shuffling past her in the kitchen.

"I did want coffee, that's why I made it." Amy scooted an empty mug across the counter. "You can refill mine, though."

Jerry welcomed Amy's sarcasm as a return to normalcy after a full week of added shifts and missed meals.

"So, I've made a list," Amy began. Her enthusiasm struck a chord of dread in Jerry — her lists usually meant chores.

"A list of what?" he asked, feigning interest.

"A list of places we can go today to research the

wax embossing on the urn." Amy's zeal in finding the owners had reached new heights since the urn's return.

"OK, and here's my counter: we don't research and we hang out and watch movies all day, maybe order a pizza." Jerry's grin met Amy's raised eyebrows and he knew he was going to lose.

"OK, and here's my counter: we go research at the library because you have missed every dinner this week."

"Good compromise," he said in a teasing tone. "Let me go take a shower, and then we can go."

Jerry took his time getting ready, hoping the delay would make Amy change her mind. Instead she waited, staunch in her plan to be productive on his first day off. At first, Jerry had been excited to hear from the coroner's office earlier that week:

"Is this Jerry Curtis?"

"Yes."

"This is Deputy Coroner Jonathan Scott. I am following up on the ashes that were brought in. You and your wife are listed as our point of contact." He paused for a response but received none. "We ran a toxicology analysis that proved negative for any illicit substances and there is no DNA match to any of our missing person listings. Since we don't have the resources to run a more extensive autopsy on cremated remains, we are delivering them to the funeral home. If you and your wife want to take responsibility, you may come by the office and fill out papers and legally have the remains released to your care."

"That's excellent," Jerry blurted in spite of the somber circumstances.

"That's one word for it," Scott replied in a clipped tone. "This also makes you accountable for the $175 transportation fee."

"That's fine," Jerry said. He was excited to get the urn back, thanks to the county's lack of funding, until he turned and faced Amy and her endless supply of energy.

"Are you ready?" she asked.

"I guess so," he said with a sigh.

* * *

Giant pillars surrounded the downtown library like diligent warriors protecting a Greek palace. The white façade did little to disguise years of wear and tear.

Jerry and Amy walked past the two sets of automatic doors and into the belly of the information beast. Amy felt confident that here their questions would be answered. Jerry did not share his wife's certainty but knew his feelings were inconsequential at this moment. This was his penance for bailing on her all week.

"So, where should we start?" Amy asked with a grin.

"I don't know; you have the list. Besides, who goes to libraries any more, anyway?"

"Smart people go to libraries," Amy snapped.

She approached the reference desk, newly hushed husband in tow. "Hi, I was wondering if you could help us. I don't really know where to start, but my husband and I are looking for some information on this symbol," Amy said, showing the reference librarian a crude drawing.

He eyed the symbol for a while, mulling over where to send them. "Well, if you think it might be a local symbol, I can direct you back to the Special Collections room. It has information about local history and things like that. Or, if you don't think that's the case, there's always our reference section."

"The Special Collections room sounds perfect. Thank you," Amy smiled her appreciation and went off to dredge through decades of local history.

The scavenger hunt for clues about a mysterious symbol on the urn did not turn out to be as easy as Amy had assumed it would be. They had investigated the racks and pulled all the books that seemed like they might be helpful. The volumes seemed endless—as soon as Amy ruled out one, Jerry gave her another from the pile.

"Why does Modesto have so much history?" Amy lamented.

"Better question, how is it all so well documented?"

"Yeah, it's well preserved but doesn't answer anything."

"We still have a lot more books to go through. We'll find something." Jerry's optimism threw Amy off.

"Look at you enjoying my idea. What a shock," she said.

"Look at you enjoying being right. What a shock."

In spite of their playful tone, the tower of books was beginning to take on an ominous feel.

"How are we going to get through all these?" Amy asked.

"Don't worry. This book looks like a winner," Jerry said, pulling a random encyclopedia from the middle of the stack like a Jenga block. The tower swayed but remained in place. Amy plucked a history in photographs from the top and they both went back to perusing the pages.

"Holy...Amy, you won't believe it."

"Shut up."

"No, seriously," Jerry said, pointing at a picture of two men holding an urn and looking solemn, the way everyone looked in the late 19th century. Even in black and white, the photo clearly was of "their" urn.

"What does it say about it?" Amy pressed.

"I haven't gotten to it yet. I just saw the picture."

"Should we make a copy of it?"

"Yeah, probably," Jerry answered. "Do you have 10 cents?"

Amy was fishing around in her wallet when her phone started ringing. She didn't recognize the phone number but answered anyway.

"Hello, is this Amy?"

"This is she. Who is this?"

"This is Chuck. We met at the bar in Oakdale the other week."

"Oh, Chuck, yes, hi!"

"Hi, I was just calling to say I talked to the owner, and he didn't have a whole lot of information about the symbol."

"Oh, really? Man, I had hoped for a better outcome with that. We are actually at the library right now researching it."

"Oh, sorry, I didn't mean to interrupt—" Amy cut Chuck off before he could offer to call back another time.

"Don't be silly. I appreciate you calling me at all. We are going to leave here soon, anyway, now that we've found something."

"Oh, you did? Anything interesting?"

"Potentially. We kind of just stumbled onto a picture, but haven't examined it yet. Why don't you come over for dinner tonight and look with us?"

"Oh, no, I wouldn't want to put you out."

"It's no trouble. It'll be my way of saying thanks for snooping around for us. We'll see you tonight at 6." Amy rattled off her address to Chuck and hung up. Jerry eyed her, waiting to be let in on whatever plans she had just made for them.

"So, I take it someone is coming over for dinner tonight," Jerry said after Amy didn't meet his gaze.

"Chuck, that guy I told you I met at the bar, he called to say he asked the owner of the bar and it's a dead end."

"Oh, then why did you invite him to dinner?"

"He's lived around here a lot longer than we have. I thought he might be helpful in putting some of the pieces together."

Jerry nodded and went off to look for the copy machine.

* * *

Amy pretended not to notice how late Chuck was. She dismissed his apologies with a wave of her hand, saying it was no big deal.

"I appreciate you two having me over for dinner."

"We appreciate you coming," Amy said as she walked to the kitchen to put dinner on the table.

The small talk continued longer than anyone wanted. Jerry finally ended the awkward weather-and-weekend-plans conversation by pulling out a collection of photocopied sheets.

"This is what we managed to gather at the library," he said.

"Yes, let's get to it," Chuck said, his excitement contagious. Amy stopped eating and looked at the papers Jerry had fanned onto the table. They each picked one to read and were absorbed instantly. They read and reread the articles, trying to tease out some clue that might have been overlooked.

"This is all so interesting," Chuck said, breaking

the silence. "May I see the urn?"

"Oh yeah, we just got it back today," Jerry said, hopping up to get it.

He carried it into the dining room, gripping it tight. His fingertips had turned white and he was taking slow, calculated steps as if he were walking down the aisle at a wedding. His concentration showed in the creases on his forehead.

"Wow, that's beautiful," Chuck said, admiring the urn as Jerry rotated it to show him the intricate designs and different angles.

Amy looked up from a piece of paper and yelped, "Here!" Jerry and Chuck's attention was ripped away from the antique. "It says the urn is made with real ivory, amethyst, and pearl and that it was created for William Chapman Ralston's ashes after his untimely death."

"Who is William Chapman Ralston?" Jerry asked sheepishly.

"Modesto's namesake, sort of," Chuck answered. "They were going to use his last name, but he asked them not to, thus proving his modesty, which is what Modesto means in Spanish."

"However," Amy said, calling the attention back to her findings. "However, the urn was stolen before it could be used. It was valued at $400 in 1870 and is estimated that today it is worth 30 times that amount!"

"Thirty times? Geez. This is one helluvan urn." Chuck said, his eyes wide.

"Yeah, and this book isn't even current. It was

written back in the 1970s or something. It has to be worth even more now." Amy's palpable glee made Jerry laugh.

"Maybe that's why that guy called us, claiming to be an heir to it," he said.

"What guy?" Chuck asked, concern in his voice.

"Oh, just some guy. He called me to say he found our information from the Sheriff's Department and that the trailer and urn belonged to him," Jerry answered nonchalantly.

"That doesn't sound good. If this urn is as valuable as this book says, you should be extra careful. Do you want me to take it for you? I have a really secure safe in my house."

"No, I think it's OK. I've got a pretty good hiding place here," Jerry said. He tried to sound reassuring, but a note of insecurity crept in.

"OK, if you're sure."

"Yeah, thanks for offering, though."

"No problem." Chuck glanced at his watch. "Nine o'clock already?"

"Oh, wow, I didn't realize it was that late," Amy said.

"I guess we were just having too good of a time. How about I take you guys out for some dessert? I've had a hankering for ice cream ever since I got into town. It's the least I can do after the wonderful dinner," Chuck said, his earnest tone winning Amy over.

"Sure. The Ice Cream Company is just down the way. Jerry?"

"Yeah, that sounds good. You two go over in Chuck's car. I'm going to lock up."

Jerry tidied up his photocopies then locked both locks. As he started down the walkway, Jerry felt a heaviness in the air, making him uncomfortable. His eyes darted around, but he saw nothing. He even walked back to double check that he had locked the door before getting into his car.

Amy and Chuck had ordered by the time he arrived. They sat patiently, awaiting their treats, trying to avoid talking about the urn and symbol. But they ended up there regardless. It was like moths to a flame—they couldn't help but let themselves be pulled back into discussing all the details of the trailer and the urn and speculating about who could be inside.

"But who could have just taken it?" Amy would ask.

"I don't know," the men would respond.

Chuck appeared to be as clueless as they were, but enjoyed playing detective. The three ate their ice cream pensively, contemplating possible answers between breaks in the conversation.

"And how did it wind up in a trailer?" Amy would ask, new question at the ready.

"I don't know," Jerry or Chuck would respond, again.

The ice cream session went on like this until they neared the last spoonfuls. Chuck went to pay while Amy and Jerry collected their phones and their thoughts.

"Well, I had a great time," Chuck said warmly as they walked out.

"Yeah, thanks so much for the help. It's always good to have another head in the mix," Amy said.

"Well I don't know how much good my head will be, but I'm always happy to help," Chuck said, waving goodbye. He got into his truck and turned toward Oakdale.

"He seems really nice," Jerry said on the drive home.

"Yeah. I like him."

They were quiet as they drove, enjoying the warm night. The house looked welcoming as Jerry pulled into the driveway. Amy waltzed up the walk.

"Did you not lock the door?" she called to Jerry, who was coming up behind her.

"What? Yes I did. I locked both locks. I even double checked."

"Why is it ajar, then?"

Alarm flashed across both of their faces. Jerry barked at Amy to stay outside and call the police, then tiptoed into the foyer. Paper littered the floor, drawers had been pulled out and their contents ripped through. Jerry followed the trail to the garage, his panic rising. He scrambled for the door and tore it open. There she sat, their little teardrop trailer, just as dinged up as she had been. He felt relief, followed quickly by fear that whoever wanted that urn now knew where they lived.

"Jerry?" Amy yelled from the front porch.

"I'm in the garage," he said. "It's OK. You can

come in."

Amy stepped delicately through the debris field their house had become. She peered into drawers to see if anything had been taken. All seemed to be in order.

"Is the trailer OK?" Amy asked in a squeaky voice.

"Yeah."

"What about the urn?"

"The urn is fine," Jerry answered. "After you two left, I decided to put it in the trunk of the car. Chuck kind of spooked me on it being dangerous here."

Amy exhaled and then looked around. "The cops said they'd be here shortly to take a report."

"OK."

"Maybe we should call Chuck and let him know what happened," Amy suggested.

"Yeah, I was thinking the same thing." Jerry was rattled. Amy could tell from his voice.

She stepped out of the garage to make the phone call and was back before Jerry noticed she'd left. "He didn't seem surprised—especially now that we know how valuable the urn is. He offered to come back and pick it up, but I told him not tonight. Too many things are going on."

Jerry nodded his head absently as Amy rubbed his arm, trying to soothe him. "Yeah," he murmured. The couple stood awkwardly, waiting for the police to arrive.

Chuck looked at the phone after hanging up with Amy. His fingers punched out a number.

"Hey Bob, it's Chuck. The urn is close." There was a pause on the other end.

"Thanks for that," a man hissed. He hung up the phone and set it on the diner counter in front of him.

"Miss, may I have my check, please?" the man asked, beckoning coolly to the waitress. He held up his card before she could even set the bill down.

When she returned, she laid the card and receipts on the counter. "Thank you, Robert. We look forward to seeing you again."

The man walked out the door, leaving his signed bill behind him — R.R., with the Rs mirroring each other.

CHAPTER SEVEN
Julia Washington

Amy lay in bed flat on her back, one arm wrapped around her head. She twirled her hair between her fingers. She hadn't felt settled since giving the officer her account of what had happened.

The full moon lighted her bedroom enough that she could see all the details of her bedroom ceiling, every speck of dirt and cobweb staring back at her. She inhaled deeply, trying to calm herself. She closed her eyes, hoping as she exhaled that her worry would go out with her breath.

No such luck. Amy's eyes whipped open. Her clock threatened her with its 2:47 a.m. reading. In less than four hours she had to start getting ready for her day. She began to shake her foot under the sheets. Something wasn't right. She inhaled again, this time forcing her hands and feet to stop moving. As she exhaled, her body slowly restarted its anxious movements. Jerry shifted next to her. She did not want to wake her husband. An overworked and under-rested

Jerry was the last thing she wanted.

The break-in had been traumatic; the police had taken statements from both of them. Apparently no one in the neighborhood had seen anything suspicious. Jerry didn't believe it. He was convinced they had some of the nosiest neighbors around. They all conveniently took the night off from snooping when something finally did happen on their street?

Images of the mess came flooding back to Amy. Copies of the photos they had found at the library were scattered all over the floor, silverware spilled out around her kitchen. Cabinet doors were open. Nothing was missing, just rifled through.

Even though Amy had declined Chuck's offer to turn around and get the urn, he'd still returned to their house when she told him what had happened. Amy initially thought it was kind of him, but now it was just another worry. Chuck hadn't been too willing to help when the police were there. He'd arrived shortly after the responding officer and Amy noticed that he'd waited in his car for some time before walking up to the house. When the police had asked to speak with him, he'd seemed hesitant. He had told them he'd seen and heard nothing.

Once the police were gone, Chuck offered again to take the urn for safekeeping. When Amy and Jerry declined, he grunted his displeasure and left abruptly. Amy thought he'd acted rude but Jerry didn't seem to notice anything odd about Chuck's behavior.

She was troubled by her thoughts. She wanted

to silence her mind but couldn't. Some stranger calls, claiming he is the owner of the trailer. What was his name? Bob? The deputy never wrote a report so how could this Bob person have found out we have the trailer? Maybe Mario and Tracy talked about it? Maybe someone from the bar overheard us talking to Chuck? It is pretty convenient timing ... but is it just coincidental? I can't believe the urn is worth so much. Someone must definitely be searching for it. Chuck was there when we found out the value of the urn. Then shortly after that the house is broken into. What's Chuck's story? Who is he? Why is he so interested in helping? Should we have trusted him? How does he know so much about this town's history? Or, maybe, WHY does he know so much? If it was about the urn, then will whoever wants it be back for it? Does Ralston have any family or something to do with the urn? Maybe this Ralston is one of the Rs on the imprint. I need to learn more about him. I think there was a picture of him at the Velvet Grill. I wonder if there is something similar at the library or maybe the McHenry Museum. Or maybe Ralston Tower? And I don't recall seeing anything related to "Ralston" in the trailer. Maybe there is a long-lost family member searching for this urn. Maybe the urn was stolen to begin with. The photo was from 1870; 127 years later the urn goes missing and we just happen to find it in a teardrop trailer? I wonder if Jerry is still planning on going to one of those gatherings. Maybe there's a connection to Ralston and the McHenrys that isn't well known. Maybe the couple was a pair of drifters. Maybe Mr. and Mrs. T.O. stole the urn? Maybe they...

"AMY!" She jerked the sheets close to her body. "What is wrong with you?" asked Jerry. "You're shaking the whole bed."

She sighed. "I just don't like it, Jerry. I don't like knowing that someone was in our home — broke into our home," Amy's hands clenched into fists on the sheets.

"I know, but the urn is safe," Jerry said.

"Right. But whoever broke in doesn't know that. What if they come back? I've been home alone a lot lately, Jerry."

Now it was his turn to sigh. "I know, dear. I'm sorry. Hopefully it won't be for much longer."

"That's not the issue now." Amy paused. "Do you think we did the right thing by keeping the urn?"

"I do," Jerry said. "Why? Are you worried?"

"I don't know if I am worried. I'm feeling unsettled. I just don't know if the urn is safe here."

The couple lay in silence for a moment.

"I think it's OK to feel unsettled after a break-in," Jerry said, trying to comfort Amy.

"I think I'm going to go back to the library after work tomorrow," she said, dismissing his effort.

"OK, do you want me to come with you?"

Amy didn't answer right away. "No, I can go on my own. Maybe I'll call Tracy to see if she can come."

"Good." Jerry kissed her on the cheek. "Now, get some rest." He rolled over and went back to sleep.

In the morning, Amy struggled to get out of bed. Her mind never had quieted enough for her to fully rest. Jerry suggested she call in sick, but she refused. She didn't want to use any sick time unnecessarily these days.

Her mind wandered back to the diary as she shuffled through getting ready for the day. It had been awhile since she'd looked through it. She decided she needed to take the diary and the notes she and Tracy had made with her to the library. Maybe she could cross-reference any information she might stumble upon.

Amy called Tracy, hoping she'd be free to join her at the last minute. While the phone rang, she opened the cabinet and reached for the diary.

"Hello?"

"Tracy. It's Amy. Do you want to---" Amy stopped midsentence.

"Do I want to what? And good morning to you, too," Tracy answered. But Amy was too busy shuffling through the cabinet for her friend's subtle jab to register.

"Amy?" All Tracy could hear was the sound of rummaging.

"Oh. My. Gosh. Where is it?" The distress in Amy's voice was clear.

"Amy?" Tracy tried again, but she didn't respond.

Amy began pulling out the contents of the cabinet and throwing them on the floor. Towels landed in bunched piles of white and teal. Boxes of batteries fell to the ground, a flashlight, sheets and blankets following.

"Amy?" Tracy said a third time. "Where's what?"

Still nothing but little sounds of panic coming from the other end.

"Amy! Are you OK?" Tracy was getting worried.

"No. I'm not OK." Amy finally answered. "It's gone."

"What's gone?" Tracy asked. No answer.

"AMY!" Tracy shouted into the phone, startling little Bianca, who was playing nearby. "Amy? Answer me. You're really freaking me out."

"The diary," was all Amy could say.

"The diary? The diary from the trailer?"

"Mmhmm."

"When's the last time you saw it?" Tracy asked. "Maybe Jerry moved it and forgot to tell you."

"I don't remember," Amy said. She looked at all of the stuff scattered on the ground around her and suddenly images of their ransacked house from the night before rushed into her mind. She sank to the floor.

Tracy didn't understand why Amy felt so panicked over the diary, but she knew her friend needed comfort.

"Amy?" she said softly. "Maybe you shouldn't go in to work today."

Her friend took a deep breath before responding. "You're right."

"Do you want to talk about what's going on?"

"Yes."

"I'm packing up Bianca and we are coming over."

* * *

"OK, start from the beginning. Tell me everything that has happened." Tracy set a mug of hot tea in front of Amy. Bianca was occupying herself with the toys her mom had brought along. Amy told Tracy about the teardrop trailer gatherings and the discoveries at the library. She detailed the encounters with Chuck. She didn't spare Tracy any details of the break-in or of her restless night.

Tracy did not interrupt her. She let her say all she needed to.

"Who would have thought this trailer would end up being so much trouble?" she asked once Amy had finished her story.

"I know. The last 24 hours have been crazy stressful," Amy said, sipping her tea. "I was thinking I would head to the library later to do some research on Ralston."

"That sounds like a good start," Tracy said, tapping the side of her mug. "Do you think Chuck's on the up and up?"

"I hope so." Amy paused. "Do you think he isn't?"

"I don't know. How important is the urn to you

and Jerry?"

"I'd like to try and return it to whoever it belongs to. I mean, wasn't that the whole point of us going to that bar? And Jerry and me going to the library?"

"Well, yeah, "Tracy said. "But what's the likelihood you will actually find out who the urn rightfully belongs to?"

Amy sat quietly for a moment. "Tracy, how long have you lived in Modesto?"

"My parents moved here in the '70s."

"Mine did, too. I remember my mother was slightly disappointed she never got to experience the 'original' library. She always loved that building."

"Oh, what's now the McHenry Museum," Tracy said.

"Right. Do you think the McHenrys and Ralston have anything to do with each other? Do you think their paths ever crossed?"

"I don't know. I'm not too knowledgeable on Modesto history," Tracy said. "I do have a friend who is a docent at the museum. She might be helpful. I can give her a call to see when she'll be there again."

"That's a great idea, Tracy. Thank you."

"I wonder if Mr. & Mrs. T.O. stole the urn. Or maybe there was a big family feud decades ago that put the urn in their hands."

"You know, I was thinking the same thing!" Amy's demeanor was more relaxed now that she had shared her worries with Tracy. "The initials are RR on the urn. I don't remember reading anything about a person in the diary whose last name is Ralston or even with R as a last initial."

"No, I don't remember seeing any of that either. But she talked about a Robert, didn't she?" Tracy turned to see if Bianca was still engrossed in her toys. Satisfied, she looked back at her friend. "I don't come across too many little boys named Robert in school."

Tracy spun her mug in small circles. "Where did you get the name Ralston, anyway?"

"From Chuck," Amy said. "The diary is from 1997? If he were a 40-something-year-old man...he would have been born in the late '40's or '50's. Robert was fairly common then, right?" Amy looked to Tracy for confirmation.

Tracy thought for a moment. "I suppose. Isn't Robert the name of the McHenry?"

"I believe so, but I'm pretty sure there's no way this could be the same guy. That Robert lived over a century ago," Amy said.

"So did Ralston, if I remember correctly. I wonder if he had any children."

Amy got up to grab something to write with and a notepad. "We should write these questions down. That way we know what we are looking for when we head back to the library."

The two women sat together writing a list of inquiries to make at the library and the museum.

Tracy scooped Bianca into her lap and snuggled with her. All the mystery was making her grateful her life was a bit more certain.

"Amy?"

"What?" she said, looking up from the notepad to meet Tracy's eyes.

"Do you think maybe the break-in had nothing to do with the urn but was about the diary?"

CHAPTER EIGHT
Dana Ardis

"She'll be there for another 45 minutes or so," Tracy said, tucking her cell phone back into her purse. "The McHenry Museum closes at 4:00."

"Great," Amy said, glancing at the clock on the kitchen wall. They'd spent most of the day reviewing her notes and speculating. Now they were going to have to wait another day to make more progress.

Tracy must have seen the look on her face. "We can make it. Come on. Besides, the library's open late, and it's right in the next block. We'll hit the museum for as long as we can and check things out at the library after."

While Tracy bundled Bianca into the car, Amy gathered up the paperwork they'd accumulated. She felt a pang for the missing diary. Illogical as it seemed, the book had felt like her link to Mrs. T. O. Without it, this hunt for more clues felt even more difficult. Then again, maybe she was just still jumpy after the break-in. She triple checked the locks on her way out.

The McHenry Museum looked just the way Amy remembered it from her field trip in elementary school. The neoclassical entryway seemed a little smaller now, but still was grand with its broad steps and imposing pillars.

Tracy's docent friend, Morgan, met them at the door. She was a friendly woman with an easy, welcoming smile and curly brown hair that showed only the slightest hint of gray.

"Half an hour is plenty of time for a tour," Morgan said, leading them past the long wooden counter where people had checked out books back when this had been the public library. "Tracy said you were interested in the McHenrys' history?"

"Yes. I've driven past this place a hundred times, but never gave it much thought. Seems like a shame," Amy said, smiling. Morgan might be perfectly nice, but the break-in had made her cautious. She and Tracy had decided to keep the true reason for this research private, just in case. No harm in being careful.

"It is a fascinating history," Morgan said, bustling them into the first of the permanent exhibits, a turn-of-the-century replica schoolroom. She was clearly in her element and glad to have an interested audience. Tracy scooped up Bianca to keep her from climbing onto one of the wooden and iron desks as Morgan began telling them about the display.

"What about Mr. McHenry's family? He had children, didn't he?" Amy asked, hoping to steer her toward information that would be more useful to her hunt.

"He had one son, Oramil," Morgan said, then told them about the young family and Robert McHenry's famous mansion. He built it, Morgan explained, so he could be closer to his job at the Modesto Bank, the first bank in town. It shortened his commute from his primary residence at Bald Eagle Ranch.

"He had a ranch?" Amy asked, drifting over to the blacksmith display, thinking of the RR seal on the urn and the identical brand burned into the planks of the H Bar B.

"Oh, yes. Over two thousand acres down along the Stanislaus River," Morgan said. "It would have been quite a ride on horseback to the bank."

"So he had his own cattle brand?" Tracy reined the conversation back around, following Amy's lead.

"He mostly had orchards," the docent said. "This area was just as good for growing fruit and the like then as it was now. He did packing, drying, all manner of processing right there at their ranch." She glanced back at the blacksmith's tools and tapped her lip, considering. "I think he had some livestock. I suppose he may have had his own brand. I don't think we have any information on it here, but there are registries for that sort of thing."

"Really?" Amy asked. Why hadn't she thought of that? That would be the perfect place to check on the brand.

"There's some sort of livestock identification bureau, I believe. It's probably somewhere under the umbrella of the Department of Agriculture," Morgan said. Then she frowned. "I doubt the McHenrys would be listed, though. They left the area in 1919 and moved to the Bay Area."

"Oh." Amy tried to hide her disappointment. She'd wanted so badly to find a local connection. None of this made sense otherwise.

Tracy wasn't so easily discouraged. "What about the Ralstons? Would they have had their own brand?"

Amy shot her a look. She hadn't wanted to bring it up so directly. Tracy shrugged, swinging Bianca over to her other hip.

"You mean William Chapman Ralston?"

At their nods, Morgan continued. "He was involved in the railroad, not in ranching around here. I really don't know about the rest of his family, of course, but he settled in San Francisco."

"I thought Modesto was almost named after him," Amy said.

"That story," Morgan said with a smile. "Modesto was built along the rail line between Sacramento and Los Angeles. Ralston was the director of the Central Pacific Railroad at the time. After famously turning down the honor of having the town named after him, he didn't have anything to do with Modesto, I don't think. He went on to be a big name in San Francisco and founded the Bank of California."

Their theories were growing thinner and

thinner. Morgan must have noticed their waning enthusiasm. "If it's that kind of history you're interested in, we do have quite an archive of local documents and photos."

Amy brightened, until Morgan added, "But we're about to close, so you'd have to come back if you want to dig through those. I can introduce you to the curator, if you'd like. Have you checked the pamphlet files in the library's Special Collections?"

"Pamphlet files?" Amy asked. When she and Jerry had gone through the local history section, they'd focused on the books.

Morgan nodded. "It has newspaper clippings, research articles, photocopies of some of the originals in our archives, things like that. You might want to check it out. They're open until 9:00 this evening."

Amy and Tracy thanked her and headed to the door with Bianca. Amy sighed as they went down the broad stone steps.

"What's that for?" Tracy asked. "I thought that went well."

"What do you mean? That was a waste of time. Ralston and McHenry weren't connected at all. And there aren't any of them left around here anyway."

Her friend laughed. "Maybe they didn't share the same suspicious cattle brand, but that doesn't mean they didn't know each other."

"How?" Amy demanded, skeptical.

"They both worked in banking. Both families ended up settling in the Bay Area. OK, that doesn't mean they were best friends or anything, but there may be a connection there that we just haven't found yet."

"I'm not driving to San Francisco to dig through their local history stuff," Amy said, rolling her eyes.

"Well, no," Tracy said. "But even if the big, famous branches of the family live out there, some of their relatives might have stayed around here. I bet if you checked the phone book, you'd find some Ralstons or McHenrys or someone related to them."

Someone with the initials R. R.? Amy wondered. She wished she knew the real initials of the trailer owner as well.

* * *

The reference librarian led the trio to the Special Collections room and unlocked it. He gave Bianca a long look, but didn't say anything. To be fair, the little girl had begun to squirm and Amy wasn't sure she'd last long in another hush-and-don't-touch-anything environment.

"These are the pamphlet files," the librarian said, pointing out a tall gray file cabinet. "The articles are arranged alphabetically, more or less. If you're interested in genealogies, you might check these, too." He pulled a couple of books off one of the upper shelves. He was tall enough to make it look effortless. Amy would have needed a step stool. No wonder she and Jerry had missed those titles.

"Also, there's the obituary index. That might be useful if you're looking for next-of-kin information," he added, one hand on the door.

"Thanks," Amy said. She wondered how much further she and Jerry would have gotten on their last trip if they'd had a better idea of where to start looking. Well, no time like the present. "Do you know anything about cattle brand indexes?"

The librarian cocked his head, thoughtful. "Not off the top of my head, but I'll see what I can find. Will you be in here for a bit?"

Amy nodded and he let himself out with a promise to check and get back to her.

Tracy sighed once the door closed. She looked like she was reaching the end of her — or maybe Bianca's — patience. "Would you mind if I take her over to the children's room for a while? I can come back."

"Go ahead," Amy said. "We don't have to stay long. I'll get an idea of what's in the files. I'd like to wait long enough to see if he can find anything about the cattle brands." She hadn't wanted to mention the specific brand, but if he could find an index, she would have a place to start.

Tracy carted Bianca off and Amy dug into the pamphlet files.

Five minutes later, she understood why the librarian had said the files were in alphabetical order "more or less." Within the folders, the clippings and documents were jumbled. The "R" folder had nothing on Ralston, to her disappointment. At first, she thought the "M" folder would be just as useless, but then she noticed that "McHenry" had an entire folder to itself.

Amy commandeered one of the tables — she could, since she was the only person in the room — and spread out a number of clippings. Articles about the mansion. Stories about the ranch and the building of the original library. She copied down any names of family and friends she came across.

Toward the back of the file, she found an entire genealogical table, four generations deep. Originally handwritten, it had been photocopied at least a couple of times and was difficult to read. She decided against trying to photocopy it again. It would be all but illegible then. Perhaps the museum's archives held the original. She looked over it, searching for double Rs. Nothing. Still nothing.

Amy was about ready to snap her pencil in frustration when the door opened. The tall librarian ducked his head in, a slip of paper in his hand.

Finally some good news. Amy tidied the stack of articles and put it back in the file. "You found the brand index?"

"Well," he hedged, "there's a copy of Cattle Brands at the Oakdale Library. We can have it sent here in a couple of days, if you'd like to look at it. The California Department of Food and Agriculture holds the index online as well, but it's not free to browse it. Some historical information is available. The 1919 Cattle Brand Index is available online here." He held out the paper.

Amy took it and read a web address in neat script. 1919. That would cover a brand that was around when the urn was first made, but would it include a symbol used to mark the wax seal? She had to hope so. She smiled and gathered her things. "Thanks. Can I get back to you about the book?"

"Of course. Just call the reference desk and we can have it sent over here for you." He held the door open for her. "Did you want to see the obituary indexes?"

Amy shook her head. She couldn't stomach the idea of any more fruitless searching right now. Tracy and Bianca needed to get home. Jerry would be home soon, too, and she had to come up with something for dinner. "Thanks, but not today."

She found Tracy and Bianca sitting next to the giant tree sculpture in the children's section. Bianca had a collection of board books spread around her, much to her delight.

"No luck?" Tracy asked.

"Well, I didn't find any solid link to the Ralstons," Amy said, trying to remind herself that it hadn't been a complete failure. She didn't have R. R.'s name, but she'd copied down a number of other names and connections from the stack of articles. Maybe the trailer owner's name would be in there somewhere, or something she could match up with T. O.'s diary. "That librarian found an online index of California cattle brands, but it's from 1919."

"Do you think the seal on the urn is that old?"

Tracy asked. She convinced her daughter to put down the last of the books without throwing a tantrum. "Let's talk about this on the way to the car. I think Bianca's about two minutes from melt-down here."

Amy followed her toward the door, flipping through her notebook. "I've got a lot of names to follow up on. Maybe one of these will turn out to be our mysterious Mrs. T. O."

"If you say so," Tracy said. She took her time strapping Bianca into her car seat. When the little girl started to cry, it seemed to crack the last bit of Tracy's patience. "None of this is getting anywhere, Amy. You don't know any more about this woman now than when you started."

Amy was tempted to agree, but she couldn't. She couldn't give this up. "No, that's not true. I know that something she had was worth stealing or our house wouldn't have been broken into. I know that something she knew was worth hiding or she wouldn't have hidden the diary. Her secrets matter."

She started the car. "Maybe we're looking in the wrong direction, trying to find out what happened one hundred years ago with this urn."

"That's where it all starts though, isn't it?" Tracy sounded tired.

"True." But that's not where it ends. Amy didn't want to push her luck. She was sure her friend would regain her enthusiasm if she didn't force the issue. When she got home, she could tell Jerry about the Cattle Brand Index and show him the notes she had from the pamphlet file. Maybe they could start on the gathering angle. Her mind spun with possibilities.

Other than Bianca's crying, it was a quiet drive home.

CHAPTER NINE
Tally Scully

"Good morning, officer. Table or booth?" the petite waitress asked, looking up at the man lumbering toward her.

"I'm actually meeting someone," he answered, no expression on his face.

"Over here, Ralph," a man in the corner booth said, motioning him to the table with a wave of his hand.

The deputy scanned the room for familiar faces as he sauntered over. He slid awkwardly into the booth, working to negotiate the many items on his utility belt into the tight space.

"Morning, Bob," he said, a slight smile on his otherwise stoic face.

"What's the word? I haven't heard from you," Bob said sharply.

"The natives have been restless," Deputy Radcliff replied with a smirk, a reference to the numerous gang-related and vagrancy complaints he answered daily.

"Shocker," Bob replied, raising an eyebrow as he stirred more milk into his coffee.

"Just as you suspected, the key was in the urn. What luck that I took the call about the trailer," Radcliff said, shifting on his seat. "I fudged a bit with the coroner and told him that the couple had opened the urn like idiots and he seemed to buy it. He didn't find anything telling when he examined the ashes, according to his report."

"What did he tell the couple?" Bob prodded.

"There was really nothing to tell. No DNA match. No traceable drugs. The coroner released the ashes to a funeral home and the couple picked them up last Friday. It should be a dead end."

"How did they react to the break-in?"

"That totally freaked them out, especially the lady. As did your phone call," Radcliff continued, with a stern look at Bob. "Any particular reason you felt the need to call them and give them your real name? They called me to complain and I had to plead ignorance to cover my butt. I told them that no report had been filed and that I had no idea how their phone number got out. Lame, man. Really stupid."

"Yeah, I got impatient. Sorry about that. It was a mistake," Bob said, looking down. "I thought it was worth a try to get the trailer back without resorting to petty theft. When you called me to tell me that you had the urn in hand, it was like a light switch. Anyway, I've been keeping tabs on the couple. They're pretty ambitious. The lady's been going to the library quite a bit, and Chuck told me they've come across some photos of Ralston holding the urn and a little information. He said they didn't really know anything concrete as of last week. Hopefully they won't be able to make any connections."

"What about Chuck?" Radcliff asked. "Do you think he's solid? He called me, acting as nervous as a cat in a room full of rabid dogs about giving his statement to the MPD after the break-in. It was just a formality, for crying out loud."

"What are the chances that she'd approach him in the bar, of all people?" Bob responded. "What could I do? He's heard me talking about the family legend since I was a boy. When he called, I felt there was no other option than to include him. I sweetened the pot by offering him a portion should we ever find what we're looking for. His family has been struggling to keep the farm above water. Chuck needs the money. We're talking about a whole lot of money here. Plus, he's come in handy. If it weren't for him, we wouldn't have had the opportunity to get the diary so soon. I told him to just lie low, stay out of the way and avoid the bar. You know how Chuck gets when he drinks. Loose lips sink ships."

"What about the diary? Did you find anything of interest?"

"No, it was pretty degraded, though it did have one page that had been carefully removed," Radcliff said. "I thought for sure that's where it would be, but we're just working with what information our family's passed down over the generations. The missing piece we need has got to be in that trailer somewhere.

"We'll find a way to get into it," Radcliff continued, glancing at his watch. "I've got to get going. I'll be in touch with a plan to gain access to that trailer. See you around."

Bob watched the deputy walk away, thinking back to all of the efforts to find the urn. A resolution to this mystery has been a long time in coming. He remembered the violent confrontation between himself and the lawyer seventeen years before and thought desperate times call for drastic measures.

* * *

That day at work, Amy was pleased to get the message that the book on cattle brands she'd requested from the Oakdale Library had arrived at the Modesto Library. Perfect. I can take it home and look it over with Jer. Tracy and Mario were coming for dinner so they could go over everything together.

On her way home, she stopped by the library, then the city's offices downtown to drop off some paperwork. She smiled as she passed the Modesto Flower Clock filled with the multicolored zinnia and impatiens blooms of late summer—one of only twelve working flower clocks in the nation, she'd read recently. When she saw the time, 5:45 pm., Amy headed for home.

"Hey, Amy, out here!" Jerry called. If you can't

beat 'em, join 'em, she thought, grabbing a Heineken and stepping outside. She found Jerry in the back yard, knocking back a cold Half Dome microbrew, tongs in hand, a bowl of marinated chicken before him.

"What time are Mario and Tracy getting here?" Amy asked. She reclined on the red Adirondack chair with the comfortable striped cushion, pulling one knee close to her chest.

"They should be here any minute."

"How was your day?" she asked after taking a sip of beer.

"Good. I think they are finally going to hire a part-timer to help out at the hospital. Not that I was minding the overtime, but it was taxing."

The sound of tires in the driveway followed by slamming car doors signaled their friends' arrival. Amy greeted them at the front door. "Hi guys. Thanks for coming over tonight." She hugged Tracy and Mario and picked up a squirming Bianca. "Jerry's out back," she said with a slight jerk of her head, directing Mario outside.

"How can I help?" Tracy asked, pulling a large cache of stuffed animals from her bag to entertain Bianca.

"Everything's ready. Can you grab the salad? Bianca, can you bring your toys?" Amy watched the little girl head for the door with an armful of stuffed animals. No sooner had they crossed the back door threshold then they heard a thud and a cry from Bianca, who had face-planted onto the concrete patio.

Jerry reached her first and immediately scooped her into his arms.

"OK, let me see. You're all right," he said, rubbing the red spot forming on the little girl's face. Amy smiled at them, marveling over how quickly Jerry had reacted.

Bianca's crying subsided to whimpers that were muffled by Tracy's shirt as the little girl was transferred into her mother's arms.

"Are you sure you guys are up for this? Long nights and screaming kids?" Tracy asked in a joking tone, knowing that her friends were more than ready. "Where are you guys on the baby front?"

"We're ready. I haven't even had the chance to tell Jerry yet, but I found out this week that we've saved enough to really start the process, thanks to Jerry's overtime," Amy said.

"That's fantastic!" Jerry exclaimed, leaning in for a kiss. "The light at the end of the tunnel," he murmured softly as they hugged.

"You two are going to be great parents," Tracy said.

Mario smiled at his friends. "As I remember, the fun's in the trying."

"We may look into adoption if we aren't successful the old-fashioned way," Amy said.

"Careful with that. I've had so many friends who started the adoption process only to find out that they're pregnant," Tracy said.

"Come what may," Amy answered wistfully. She

and Jerry caught each other's eyes and shared hopeful looks.

"Not to change the subject," Mario said, "but I heard that there's going to be a Trailerfest in Lodi next week. Sounds like fun. Let me know if you need someone to go with you. What's up with the rest of the 'investigation' these days?

"Is Chuck going to be joining us tonight?" he continued with a snicker.

"No, I don't think Chuck will be coming around any more," Jerry muttered. "He seemed OK at first, but now Amy has me convinced that he acted pretty shady after the break-in. He's definitely on my radar now. I can't believe I let Amy ride alone with that guy,!

"We'll catch you guys up on the investigation fter dinner. Apparently Amy brought home some new stuff to research, if you're interested," Jerry said as he took the chicken off the grill. "Dinner is served."

After clearing the dishes, the couples reconvened around the dinner table. "Let's see if the book I picked up today has any constructive new info," Amy said, digging through the black hole she called a purse. "It's supposed to have all of the brands local to this area."

While Mario and Tracy scrolled through the online Cattle Brand Index of 1919, she and Jerry took on the Cattle Brands book.

"Honey, should we come back in a few hours when you're ready?" Amy teased Jerry. "Keep flipping," she said, impatient at his need to study every brand.

"The brands are in brandabetic order, but I'm not finding anything in the Rs," Jerry said. "Why wouldn't it be here?"

"Amy, this is it! This is the brand," Tracy exclaimed, with such gusto that Mario jumped. The four studied the brand's unique interlinking letters.

"OK, so it looks like the brand design belongs to Douglas R. Brewster and his wife, Marguerite," Amy read aloud. "It says that the property is at 960 Crawford Road, Modesto, California. There is a letter and a group of numbers beside the address and underneath the name — B 147453." Amy paused for a moment, then said, "I'm certain that the name Brewster is on the list of acquaintances, friends and colleagues that I compiled from the pamphlets at the library." She grabbed her black notebook, running her finger down the page as she looked for the name Doug Brewster. "There. Why didn't I write down the relationship to Robert McHenry as I went? Now I'll have to go back to the pamphlet files to check."

"Why don't we try cross referencing Brewster's name with McHenry's online and see what we come up with," Jerry suggested, opening a new tab on his laptop.

Tracy thought back to the diary entry she and Amy had seen what seemed like a lifetime ago. "Amy, this is the name from the diary, the one we couldn't fully read. I'm sure of it: Doug and Mar_____. Finally, a connection to the diary! Mrs. T.O. and the Rolling Ranch owners obviously were within the same social circle."

"Do you guys realize we now have a concrete, tangible lead? " Amy asked, unable to look away from the computer screen.

"If that excites you, wait until you read this Bee article," Jerry said. He swiveled his laptop around for her to read.

"You've got to be freaking kidding me," Amy said as she read the headline: Brewster Mansion? Historian finds evidence Robert McHenry wasn't a McHenry. "This article suggests that Robert McHenry was born Robert Henry Brewster. Could that be true? How did I not hear about that and why didn't the docent at the McHenry Mansion mention it? I guess I wasn't asking the right questions."

Jerry seemed as stunned as Amy. "If this article is true, we may have a family connection with Douglas and Marguerite Brewster. It says that Robert was originally from Ohio but came out here to reinvent his persona after deserting the Army when directed to the front lines of the Mexican-American War. The reporter found evidence in an 1860 census that McHenry lived with a Brewster who turned out to be his brother. If one of his family members made it out here to California, do you think it's possible that others may have, too? Maybe a cousin or uncle?"

"This is going to help with this weekend's search in the Special Collections Room," Amy said, flashing a huge smile. "Since you don't have to work this Saturday."

"Great," Jerry retorted sarcastically. His smiling

eyes said it all, though. He was excited, too.

The next day, he and Amy visited the Modesto Library again. "I can't wait to bring our kids here," she said as they watched parents guiding their kids into the Children's Room. Jerry noticed his wife touching her belly, a new habit of late.

They were escorted into Special Collections, with its quiet and serious air. Gone were the sounds of children and parents having fun. It was time to get down to business.

Amy knew what she was looking for and felt optimistic that this trip to the library would be fruitful. Genealogy. Land title information. Parcel maps.

"We're back," Amy said to the now familiar librarian. "The online cattle brands index was a great find. Now I am armed with a name. I need to see the McHenry family genealogy. I'm also looking for land titles and property parcel maps today. Would I find those here?"

"Genealogy-related items, yes," answered the librarian. "For land titles and maybe for parcel maps, you're going to have to go to the Clerk Recorder's office."

"What do we do now?" Jerry asked as they stepped aside to redirect their efforts. "Do you want me to head down there?"

As he spoke, Amy's phone vibrated in her purse. Embarrassed, she fumbled to answer, wishing she had turned the phone off.

"Hi, Tracy," she said softly. "What's up?"

"Don't be mad, Amy, but I've been keeping my docent friend, Morgan, in the loop about the Brewster connection. I described the brand to her and wanted to see if there was more information about whether the name bore any connection to McHenry. She called me this morning with a tip. Morgan was helping a student research some McHenry files in the museum's collection yesterday and came across a folder with the Rolling Ranch brand. She mentioned that it contained a map. She photocopied it and is working at the museum today if you want to pick up the material.

"Amy, I think it would be well worth your time to get over there if you can."

"Wow! Are you serious? OK. We're at the library right now. I'm reviewing the McHenry file at the library, trying to find the article where I first saw Douglas Brewster's name, but it looks like Jerry is available," Amy said. "Let me ask him if he's willing to walk over there to check it out. Great work, Tracy! And, no, I'm not mad at you. Thanks for getting involved. Will you call her back and let her know that Jerry's on his way?"

"Sure thing, Amy. Love you, girl."

"What did you just sign me up for?" Jerry asked, glad for a new mission.

"All right, so I need you to walk over to the McHenry Museum and introduce yourself to Morgan. She found a piece of information marked with the RR brand in the museum's collection," Amy said. "Tracy hinted that there is something in that book that will blow our minds. You down to check it out?"

"I'm all over it!"

As Jerry climbed the museum's stairway, he felt for the first time the weight of how his and Amy's search might impact Modesto.

He approached a docent with a hesitant smile. "Hi. I'm looking for Morgan."

"You must be Jerry," she said, extending her hand. "I am so glad that you could meet me today. I think this information will help you and your wife, from what Tracy said."

He opened the file and saw a skillfully drawn map of a property — the house, a barn, the Stanislaus River, pastureland. Even though it was a color photocopy, he could tell the map was yellowed with age but reasonably well preserved. As Jerry's eyes drifted to the top right corner of the page, he saw the inverted R brand and a date, 1861. His heart beat faster as he noticed the name above the property map, Rolling Ranch, written in an old-fashioned script. He began to notice new details—a large grouping of trees on the north end of the property, small rock formations to the east. Jerry couldn't believe it when he saw the name of the neighboring ranch to the east, penned in small, almost illegible print — Bald Eagle Ranch!

His eyes met Morgan's. "Thank you for contacting Tracy. I can't wait to go through the rest of the information with my wife."

As Amy approached the car, she could see that

Jerry was excited. "Ready to go?" she asked.

"Yes!" he said, then whispered, "This map is the mother lode of good information. Did you find anything?"

"Oh, I found something all right," she said smugly.

CHAPTER TEN

Ellie Cummins

Amy felt as if she might shoot out of the car into space with excitement. Her heart was beating in a crazy, out-of-control cadence.

"There really was another child!" She gasped. "A boy. Possibly a lost heir to the McHenry fortune!" She studied Jerry's reaction.

"You're on crack," he said with a chuckle, keeping his eyes on the road.

"Jerry!" She smacked his arm and he rubbed it with a forced whimper.

"Seriously, an obituary in Special Collections. This child might be related."

"Might?" He sighed. "You mean you're not sure?"

"No, but I feel it. The article said there were twins born to an Elizabeth Rose the year of that devastating flood — near Rolling Ranch, Brewster's homestead. It just said the babies were born in a barn. One of the little boys didn't survive." She drew in a long breath and squeezed Jerry's hand. "What if there was a love story here that we just don't know about?"

"Wow," Jerry said. "One mystery at a time! The map we found in the archives shows that the McHenrys and Brewsters were neighbors, or as neighborly as you can get along the river. Bald Eagle and Rolling Ranch's lines nearly crossed. Too bad they weren't on the same river where we found my trailer."

"Our trailer!" Amy said in a high voice.

His eyes darted over to hers. "So now it's our trailer?" He beamed that infectious, lopsided smile.

"I wonder if whoever owned that diary could have known about these babies," Amy said, "or could just be protecting a secret love affair." Her face went serious. "Maybe the barn was..."

Jerry interrupted her, patting her knee. "You don't know that for sure. I have a website I need to check out that may have some more answers, but I think I'm going to take a break tomorrow for just a bit. Too much information for my brain for one day. All these names, dates, and numbers are making me want a donut or a Marie Callender's lemon meringue pie.

"Tomorrow is Sunday. I'm sleeping in before I take on more of the Great Teardrop Trailer Caper," Jerry said. "I'm losing hairs by the minute."

Amy's throat tightened as she walked up to their porch. Sleeping in did sound amazing, but the break-in was still on her mind and something else was nagging at her. That night, before switching off her bedside lamp, she settled under the covers with one of the

Better *Homes and Gardens* she'd found in the trailer. Who was Mrs. T.O. and what did she know? It was possible that the diary was missing some pages and all the answers were lost with them. She tucked the magazine beside her and drifted off to sleep.

* * *

Amy sat up in bed with a jerk and rubbed her belly. The dream had felt all too real. She'd sell her soul to erase the memories of that day many months ago. It was getting harder and harder to keep her own secrets even though she'd been pretty successful these last few months, and she did feel better about it since she and Jerry had decided it was time to start a family. This diary mystery had taken on new life since its disappearance because now she really felt drawn to understand the person whose suffering was evident in its pages — the keeper of secrets.

She had felt her own loss of a child: a failed pregnancy that Jerry had never known about. She had gotten pregnant despite the endometriosis, and the timing was all wrong back then. He was working so much and the baby fund wasn't big enough. He'd said in a year or two it would be better, but she thought well, maybe. If she handed him a box with the pregnancy test and a pair of booties inside, she thought maybe Jerry would be excited. But she miscarried a week later. It was a blessing in disguise, she supposed, but she still couldn't shake the emptiness she felt every time she dreamed of a little girl with flaxen hair and a crooked smile, pieces of both of them smiling back at her.

She hadn't even told Tracy, who she was sure would have helped her muddle through the weeks of mourning with trips to Vintage Faire Mall and Starbucks for a sympathy Mocha Frappuccino. She just wasn't in the mood for all the talking that would require. It felt safer to suffer in silence.

Now, she lay in bed thinking. What more could there be? Who was the true owner of that trailer and urn? Amy scrunched up her face and balled her hands into fists. An idea kept nagging at her, so she got dressed quickly, snatched her keys off the counter, and ran to her car.

There must have been a weekend run at Legion Park because cars were lined up out of the parking lot, almost to the road. She knew the deserted trail she and Jerry had ridden along a few weeks ago would be crowded. Crap, she thought. How could she get down to the spot without looking like a weirdo foraging through the brush and digging in the dirt when there were tons of high school kids training for cross-country teams? Luckily, her running shoes were in the trunk.

Amy paced herself so she wouldn't be worn out by the time she located the spot where Jerry had found his prized teardrop. Blend in like a ninja and try not to drop dead.

"Hello," she panted each time a runner passed

her. She felt inadequate because it was still at least a mile more down the path. More bike rides, more salads, less Heineken. And definitely no lemon meringue pie.

The spot hadn't changed a bit. The brush was just as dry and crispy as it had been the day they pulled her out of the hard dirt. Amy bent over to catch her breath; then she slowly made her way down to the spot. She began picking up rocks and weeds and tossing them to the side. Maybe another clue would jump out at her — the rest of the license plate would be nice. Maybe the diary would appear suddenly out of thin air. Crazy talk.

Amy heard the sound of feet pounding the ground every few minutes. She thought she was hidden in the brush when a voice from above made her flinch so hard that the tree behind her shuddered.

"Did you lose something?" It was a young man's voice.

Amy struggled to stand up. With the help of a dead tree, she pulled herself back up to the trail.

"Hi." She cleared her throat. "My keys flung out of my pocket, but I found them." She pulled them from her shorts pocket and jingled them.

"Awesome!" The man jogged in place for a few beats and then stopped. "You know there was something out here once but now it's gone. Some weird, old-fashioned trailer thing, I guess.

"Oh yeah?" Amy answered, her throat dry.

"There was a man poking around here just a few minutes ago," the jogger said. "He stopped me in the parking lot to ask if I'd seen it or anybody looking over here."

"Was he from the Police Department? Maybe it was stolen and dumped."

"No," he said, wiping his forehead with his wrist. "I don't think so. Maybe a rancher. He took off in a small red truck. He looked upset."

Amy stared off over the jogger's shoulder and wondered how fast she could get to her car and try to find the truck.

"What makes you think he was a rancher?"

"Had a double R brand sticker in his window."

Amy shifted her feet, her mind whirling.

"Well, got my keys," she said. "Gotta finish my run before I'm out of steam!" She forced a smile, waved at the man and started running toward her car.

Her head pounded as she pressed down on the gas pedal. She felt so frustrated. Jerry wanted that trailer. No, he needed that trailer, and she'd been so testy with him lately. Chuck's eagerness to take the urn off their hands had made her uneasy and she felt overly protective of the diary. It fell into my lap for a reason, Amy thought. She worried about it as if it were crying out for her help, as silly as that seemed. But after all, her Nana had said if something was loved once then it had a soul — even an inanimate object. Whoever was in that urn should be placed in his or her final resting place if they could ever figure out who it was. But the vessel might get a pretty penny at auction.

Selfish, she scolded herself, pushing her sweaty bangs off her face. How dare she think of monetary gain at a time like this? Her tattered little book of secrets knew who was in that urn and whoever stole that diary knew it, too. Was there something else inside the trailer that they hadn't found? Maybe the thieves suspected that she and Jerry had it. Who did this and what was their motive? And where in the name of God was that red truck?

Amy whizzed past the slow cars in front of her, taking care not to exceed the speed limit that much. She looked around at every red light to see if she could spot the red truck. Nothing.

Instead of going straight home, Amy decided to drive by the cemetery. She slowed down as she approached Acacia Memorial Park with its bumpy rock walls and nicely manicured lawns. She smiled when she thought of the majestic old trees standing watch over the dead, including her grandparents. Amy's grandmother had chosen a plot next to the grandest tree that made Amy think of her Nana in her false eyelashes, glitzy clip-on earrings and sparkly hats. Thank you, she thought to the spirits in the air, for giving me a reason to smile when I drive by this place.

Then she saw it. Parked along one of the roads in the cemetery sat a red truck with a sticker on the back window. A man was hunched down next to a grave. Amy turned right into the parking lot of the clinic across the street, turned around and headed back to the cemetery. Her heart was beating fast.

She slowed down when she entered, avoiding four cats that scurried into her path. Amy wondered why so many cats wandered the cemetery but then realized there was a house at the entrance. Maybe the owners fed them.

Sadness washed over her as she remembered Nana's funeral, but then she shook it off. Focus. Which road was it? She drove through the cemetery but saw only a small blue car and a man on a riding lawnmower.

"Excuse me," Amy called, straining to be heard over the racket. "Sir?" This time she waved at the gardener. He turned off the mower and said, "Yes, ma'am?"

"Did you see that red truck parked right here?"

"Yes, ma'am."

"Do you know whose grave site he was visiting?"

The man dabbed his neck with a handkerchief. "No I don't, and even if I did it wouldn't be my business to tell you."

He looked around and then hopped off the seat. "These plots over here don't all have stones, but you can take a look right about .... there." He pointed his finger to an area near the exit onto Scenic Drive, close to the Pioneer section of the cemetery.

"Thank you so much, sir," Amy said. "You've been a great help." She pulled her car up a few yards and turned it off. She walked past the graves with dried-up carnations in faded colors of red, white and blue and felt sorry to see many with no flowers. Others had fresh lilies and narcissus in plastic vases, ribbons flitting in the breeze. These were the dead who were not forgotten.

As Amy approached a small plot with only a tiny metal numbered marker, her hands flew to her mouth. A small cow sat next to the marker. It wasn't like the Fisher-Price farm animals she and her cousin Jack had played with when they were kids. This toy was older. She looked around and then bent down beside the grave and tenderly picked it up. An "R" was scratched into its underside.

So many thoughts buzzed inside her head it started to ache. Amy got back into the car and clenched the steering wheel tightly. She dumped the contents of her purse onto the seat, rummaging for her cell phone as she tried to slow her breathing and control her trembling.

Before she could make her call, the phone rang.

CHAPTER ELEVEN

Doug C. Souza

"Do exactly as I say, or your husband Jerry dies," the voice on Amy's cell phone commanded.

She pulled it away from her ear, as if it were a snake about to strike. Amy double-checked the incoming ID to confirm it: the call came from Jerry's phone.

"How'd you...what do you want?" she asked, returning the phone to her ear.

"First, make sure I'm not on speaker, and then tell me where you are," the voice said.

"You're not on speaker, and I'm at a cemetery."

"Get to your car."

"I'm already in my car."

The voice sighed. "You're sitting in your car at a cemetery? Weird."

"I just got in. I was leaving. Who is this?" she asked warily.

"This is the guy who's got a gun to your husband's temple and would rather not have to spray

124

bits of his brains all over your gaudy living room. Yellow and blue canvas sectional, really, what were you thinking?"

"He's okay," Amy sputtered, falling back into the driver's seat. "Is he okay?"

"For now," a pause. "Jerry, say 'hello.'"

Amy listened carefully. There was a shuffling noise and then Jerry calling out, "Amy, don't come home. Get—"

Amy heard sounds of a commotion and then Jerry crying out in pain.

The voice returned: "Sorry 'bout that. I had to put three shots into your couch and press the heated barrel against Jerry's neck. The steel gets extra-hot when a silencer's attached — burned him something fierce. Seems Jerry wanted to go all heroic on us. Couldn't have that."

Amy choked back a sob. She blinked hard, trying to figure out her next move. "What do you want?" she asked through gritted teeth.

"Hey, don't get all hotty-totty with me, missy. I'm trying to get to that. Are you ready to listen?"

"Yes."

"Good. Now, I figure you'll start working out a way to get help, if you haven't already. Of course, we can't have that. So, are you in your car?"

"Yes."

"Good. Put me on speaker so I know you aren't flagging anyone down or making some pointless attempt to call the police. You're going for a drive. By the way, if I hear anything suspicious, I shoot Jerry."

Amy sucked in a deep breath. "Where?"

"Well, I'll start with a knee or something, but if you screw around, I'll gut him."

"No, you monster, where do you want me to go?"

"Oh, of course. You're coming home to join us. Now, you keep talking to me the whole drive. What cemetery did you say you're at?"

"Acacia, off Scenic and Bodem," she said, turning on the car, muting the radio, and setting her cell phone close to her on the passenger seat.

"Hmm, that's about five to 10 minutes away, I imagine. I'll give you seven to get here. Try not to get pulled over."

It took all of Amy's concentration to put the car in drive and pull out onto Scenic Drive. "Tell me what you want. You don't need to hurt him."

"Oh, good topic of conversation for our little drive here," the voice chuckled. "I was worried I'd have to make small talk about your wretched taste in floral patterns. Really, daisy embroidered pillows on paisley upholstery? Where do you even find paisley-infested furniture anymore? Anyway, what do I want?"

The cell phone went quiet. Amy grabbed it, worried she had lost the signal. A car honked as she swerved into the oncoming lane. "Hello? Hello?" She yanked the wheel back and steadied her nerves.

"I said don't get pulled over. Sounds like a sound effects CD out there. Anyway, my associate and I would like nothing more than to hitch up this damned teardrop camper and be outta here, but you and your Scooby-Doo husband had to empty the thing out."

Amy scanned the packed parking lot at Save Mart. *All those people, if I could just let one of them know.* "We can put it all back. We didn't know," she said, returning her gaze to the road ahead.

"Well, that's neither here nor there. You think I like hurting people? Ol' Jerry here was locked up, didn't say anything. Lucky for him, he got a text in the middle of our interrogation and my associate had the brilliant idea to call you."

Amy took a deep breath and blinked hard, erasing the tears. She was close to home and would need all her wits. "Okay, so tell me what you're looking for and I'll give it to you."

"Well...that's the problem. I can't say it straight out because then I'd be giving too much away. I'd rather find that middle ground where you tell me everything and I figure out if you and Jerry here are useful enough to keep alive."

"So what then? What do we do?" Amy asked, turning onto her street. A white unmarked sedan was parked in front.

"Well...ah, my associate tells me you're pulling onto the street. I'll let you know how you can help once you're in here. Remember, don't you dare hang up. I don't want any funny tricks where you dial 911 and leave the line open. I've seen 'Matlock" The voice paused. "Besides, it looks like you've got company.

Time to take me off speaker."

Amy did so and put the phone to her ear as she pulled into the driveway.

Andreas stood in his flip-flops and bathrobe, waiting on her front porch. The 68-year-old blocked the path to the front door.

* * *

Andreas didn't like what he saw. Amy was a harried mess, giving him a forced smile and a wave as she stepped out of the car. Her keys jangled as she tried to set the auto-lock. It took several tries.

This didn't bode well with what Andreas had seen 20 minutes earlier: two guys arguing as they approached the Curtis' front door. About 15 minutes later, he thought he had heard a yell from inside.

No one had answered the door when he knocked.

Andreas rubbed the bridge of his nose. Maybe he should've called the cops straight away, but he had been warned about anymore "conspiracy theories" or "wild-goose chases." His last fine for a false alarm from the MPD had shot past triple digits. Even his beloved Rose agreed with the officer that jail time might be necessary after the next infraction. Actually, she had insisted that they take him away that afternoon.

He pictured the cops showing up and finding three guys watching some sports game. But now, Amy strode toward him as though she were concentrating on every step.

"No, he's our neighbor," she muttered into the phone. "He's fine. Please, yes, I'll handle it." She glanced up and beamed an eerily forced smile. "Hi, Andreas, what can I do for you?"

"Uh, just ... wanted a cup of sugar," he said. "Everything okay?"

"Sure, sure, everything's fine." She held her keys out to unlock the door, and then turned the doorknob, as if remembering it already was unlocked. "Sorry, we don't have any sugar." She kept the phone plastered to her ear.

"You don't have any sugar?" Being well-versed in the thespian arts, Andreas recognized a poorly improvised line when he heard one.

"No, um, I know because we just ran out and I was supposed to pick some up. See you later, gotta go." Amy shut the door in his face.

"No problem," he yelled through the door. "You have a good day." The hairs on the back of Andreas' neck stood up. After years of watching over the neighborhood, his day had come: He was needed.

But how to proceed?

Intel. He needed to gather intel.

Andreas summoned his teachings from the *The Way of the Samurai*: There is nothing more than the single purpose at the present moment.

After taking a deep breath, he tiptoed the best he could in flip-flops past the driveway and into the side yard. He lifted the gate handle, crept in, and crouched down.

Nothing in the garage, laundry room, or kitchen.

Ooh, Jer's a propane guy. I woulda taken him for a charcoal guy. Andreas examined the high-end Char-Broil grill, wondering why he'd never been invited to a backyard barbecue.

"Focus!" Andreas admonished himself.

He heard muffled voices farther along; they were in the living room. The sliding glass door was shut, but the bay window was cracked open — typical for this time of year. Every shade was drawn, so he couldn't see anything.

Andreas' robe got caught on a rosebush thorn as he crawled toward the window. He tugged it loose, scraping his wrist in the process. Like a true samurai, he didn't make a peep. He leaned in and his left thigh cramped. Again, no sound as he winced, stretched his leg, and shook out the cramp.

I am a samurai.

With an ear just below the window screen, he listened.

"Show her the vid," someone said. "You should recognize the person I'm talking to, your pal Deputy Radcliff. It's a cell phone recording that I had Chuck here sneak, so you'll excuse the audio. However, if you listen carefully, you'll hear him talk about how he's been lying to you, how he figured the break-in would freak you out.'"

"You, too, Chuck?" Amy asked.

"Leave Chuck out of this," the stranger said.

"The point is — I've got Deputy Radcliff, which means I've got the cops. These coincidences of yours where you pop up everywhere at the wrong time are starting to annoy me. I've got something to find and you're gonna help me find it."

Andreas nodded to himself: Smart, not calling the fuzz.

"How do we know you won't just kill us?" Jerry asked. At least it sounded like Jerry.

Good question, Jer, Andreas thought.

"You don't," the stranger said matter-of-factly. "But I could shoot you in the kneecaps to make sure you help me."

"This is too much, Bob," a new voice said. *Chuck?* "This is steamrollin' outta control."

"First, shut the hell up, Chuck. Second, shut the hell up. And third, you are hired help. Don't forget your place."

"I'm walking, man," Chuck said. "I'm walking away."

"Don't move another inch," Bob said. "Forget about what Radcliff can do to you. Think about this Glock for a second. Think about what it will do to you. You're a cowboy. I'm sure you've seen what a bullet does to a slab of meat."

"I won't go no farther with this," Chuck said.

"Fine."

Three muffled pops sounded, followed by a crash.

Amy screamed.

"Shut up! Shut up or Jerry's next," Bob yelled. "Now, no more playing around."

Andreas couldn't agree more: No more playing around. He slinked away, got to the side gate, cinched up his robe, and prepared for action. As the great Jim Morrison sayeth, "The time to hesitate is over."

* * *

Jerry stared at the prone body. Chuck lay face down, his breathing shallow. Blood pooled at his abdomen. Jerry continued to pull at the duct tape on his wrists and ankles.

"Get up," Bob ordered and moved to lift Jerry off the couch. "We're going to your garage and finishing this blasted errand."

The little fat man was having trouble hefting and holding his gun at the same time. Jerry considered rushing him, but the guy kept the gun locked on Amy. His fear had turned to anger the moment Bob started pointing that damned pistol at her. First chance he got, he'd rip the guy's throat out.

A knock at the front door jolted all of them.

"Ignore it," Bob said as Jerry gingerly stepped away from the couch.

The knocking grew louder and more insistent.

"Are you expecting anyone?" Bob asked them.

"No," Amy said, her voice quivering.

Bob pressed the gun to Jerry's temple.

"No," Amy insisted.

Jerry leaned away from the gun and shook his head.

The knocking continued. "I really, really need to talk to you." It was Andreas.

Bob sighed. "Get rid of him, now, now, now," he ordered Amy.

Jerry watched as she went to the door, calculating his chances of spinning and slapping the gun away with his bound hands before it went off.

Bob had kept his finger firmly pressed against the trigger the entire time. Six shots, Jerry remembered, three in the couch, three into Chuck, but how many does a Glock clip carry?

"Andreas, what are you doing?" Amy asked as she backed into the living room.

Jerry's jaw dropped at the image before him: Andreas, clad in his usual robe and flip-flops, walking into the room with a pistol drawn and pointed squarely at Bob.

Bob shifted so he was behind Jerry and aimed his gun at Andreas.

"Put down the Glock," Andreas said. Wet dirt stains streaked his robe. At least Jerry hoped it was wet dirt.

Bob laughed, "Not what I expected. Anyway, why don't you put the gun down?"

"Why don't you?" Andreas asked in a measured tone.

Oh God, he's playing a character, Jerry worried.

"Or no, how about we stand like this until

someone fires? Or we stand like this all day? What do you say?"

Andreas' face remained granite. "I say this: See how I'm holding my Smith and Wesson? I've got one hand on the grip, while my other hand wraps the first. My arms are extended, my right arm straight and my left braced to stabilize my shot. Also, I noticed you shoot in three-shot increments. The couch is shot three times, as is that poor fella on the ground. Each shot is spread by at least twenty centimeters."

Jerry wondered how Andreas saw any of this, since his eyes hadn't left Bob since walking in.

Andreas continued, "Three-shot increments show a lack of ability or a lack of confidence. This Smith and Wesson will need only one shot, right where I'm pointing. Now, drop your gun."

"Yeah," Bob said snarkily, "but I've got a meat shield."

Jerry did the calculations: *Amy was to Andreas' right. Bob's Glock was just inches from his head. If he could shove Bob's arm enough to make his shot waver . . . .*

The wait was growing too tense. Something bad was going to happen, Jerry was certain. The only risk in shoving Bob's arm was that Andreas might miss his target and shoot Jerry instead.

Jerry's eyes fell on Amy. Her eyes were blurry and red. Dried streaks stained her cheeks.

She glanced his way, beseechingly.

Jerry no longer cared if Andreas accidentally shot him. At least Amy would be safe.

He lunged for the gun, digging his teeth into Bob's wrist.

The Glock puffed out shots into the ceiling. Andreas dashed forward and shot Bob square in the face.

The sound was deafening. Jerry's ears rang with a high-pitched whistle.

Bob grabbed Jerry, dragging him down.

"The gun!" Jerry yelled, realizing that both of Bob's hands gripped him. They were empty — no gun.

Tumbling backward, Jerry saw Amy and Andreas searching the floor.

"Got it," Amy yelled. Her voice sounded far away. She shoved the gun into Andreas' hand.

Bob kicked away and darted past everyone to the front door. He turned and glanced back as he pulled the door open; half his forehead was charred. Burnt ends of hair streaked the left side of his head.

Andreas stood with both guns. Amy ran to Jerry and hugged him hard. He felt her breath on his ear but only heard soft mumbles.

He kissed her. After coming up for air, he pointed to his ear. "Muh, muh, muh..." He opened his jaw wide, trying to pop his ears.

She said something, but he could only read her lips. Something that ended with "I love you."

"Can't hear too well," he hollered. "But I love you, too."

Andreas shook his head and called out, "None of us will be able to hear for a bit."

"What happened?" Amy asked. "I saw you shoot him in the face."

"Blanks," Andreas said with a shrug. "Stage gun. I stuffed some dirt in the barrel on my way over," he yelled, using his hands to demonstrate what he meant.

"On your way over?" Jerry asked, some of his hearing starting to return.

"Long story. Short version: I heard about the cops being in on it, ran home and got my gun. Er, fake gun."

"That stuff about proper gun holding or whatever you were saying?" Jerry asked. "That was freakin' awesome." He winced, the sting from the burn on his neck returning.

"A little *Rumpole of the Bailey* skit I was in at the West Side Theatre in Newman a few years back. You see, we trained for authenticity because—"

"Uh, sorry to interrupt you two, but we've got a person bleeding to death here," Amy shouted, grabbing towels from the kitchen and rushing to Chuck's side.

CHAPTER TWELVE

Loretta Ichord

Jerry and Amy collapsed on their ruined couch after the ambulance left and they'd given their statements to the police. They had Chuck's blood on their hands and on the pile of towels by their feet, but they didn't seem to notice.

"Do you think Chuck will live, Jerry?" Amy asked, her ears still ringing from Andreas' gun.

"Don't know. He lost a lot of blood."

Andreas banged a hand against his clogged ear as he shuffled back and forth across their living room. "A person could suffer a horrific death when shot in the gut. The stomach, as you know, is filled with hydrochloric acid, and when blood mixes with it, a painful toxemia ..."

"Andreas! Spare us your Dr. Gerald role. We have enough to deal with, like how to get out of this mess we got ourselves into," Jerry said, lifting his hand to his neck. He stopped when he saw his fingers. He looked at Amy's. "Geez, we've got blood all over us."

Amy snapped out of her daze. "Eck!" She rushed into the bathroom, slamming the door. Jerry and Andreas heard the shower running full steam.

Jerry started to follow her out of the living room, forgetting about Andreas. He had to protect Amy. He still couldn't believe what had happened. The three of them had nearly bought the farm and Chuck might be buying his right now. Jerry tensed at the thought of no kids, no future, all because of a little trailer. He was tempted to haul it back to the park.

"Jer, I don't know if I'd trust the fuzz," Andreas said. "Remember what that nutcase Bob said about them and this Deputy Radcliff? Who knows if they're really putting out an APB for those turkeys? We've got to do our own detective work. Find out what he wants so bad he'd murder for it." Andreas flip-flopped over to the door leading into the garage. "The teardrop; we gotta search it right now before the cops do."

Jerry whipped around. "Whoa, there, neighbor! We? What do you mean, we? I think you need to go home, Andreas. Rose must be looking for you."

Andreas hung his head low as he did an about-face. "Yeah, you're right. See you around, Jer. Keep the Smith and Wesson in case that weirdo comes back."

Jerry closed his eyes, trying to get a grip on his emotions. "Hey, wait a minute, Andreas. That was no way to speak to the man who helped save our lives." Jerry walked over and stood in front of his neighbor. "I'd give you a hug, but," he held up his bloody hands, "as you can see, I'm not able to do that right now."

Andreas grinned. "I'll take a rain check, Jer."

Jerry grinned back as Andreas opened the door and left. He'd never complain about his nosy neighbors again.

After his shower, Jerry found Amy on their bed, wrapped in her robe, staring into space.

"Get dressed, honey, and pack a few things. I'm taking you over to Mario and Tracy's to stay. It's not safe here until they catch those bad guys."

Amy didn't look at him when she asked, "What about you? You're not staying here by yourself, are you?"

"Yeah, but I'll be OK. The police said they'll have a patrol car cruise by every few hours."

"Then I'm staying. We're in this together, Jerry." Amy eyed the corner of the bedroom where she'd stacked the photos and papers from the library and museum. "It's my fault you almost got killed today. I kept pushing this research stuff," she said, pointing at the pile. "I should have left it alone." She broke down, sobbing into her hands.

Jerry sat down next to her and drew her to his chest. "No, Amy, it wasn't your fault. I was as eager as you to find out about the teardrop and the urn. But it was all those darn long hours at work that made me less than energetic. And don't forget, I'm the one who had the blame thing hauled here."

She pulled away, rubbing her swollen eyes. "OK, let's stop the blame game and take a couple of days off work. We both need the rest."

"Sounds good. It'll be payback time for Randy."

"Let's try to get some shut eye," Amy said. She and Jerry lay back on the bed and fell into an exhausted sleep.

At 3 in the morning, Jerry woke, wide-eyed and worked up. Amy snored softly next to him. He slipped quietly from the bed and threw on some clothes.

Jerry went into the garage and stared at the troublesome teardrop, questions rattling around in his head. Was Andreas right? Should they search it again before Bob, the cops, or that crooked deputy got to it? But surely Bob didn't have control over all the deputies or officers in the county. He had to be lying. Bob was definitely short a few. Whoever heard of a bad guy holding a gun to somebody's head while spouting off about ugly floral patterns?

He swung the teardrop's galley open and began to search.

* * *

"Bob, you monkey-brained idiot!" Deputy Radcliff yelled into his cell phone. "You've ruined everything and if I wasn't your long-suffering cousin, I'd sink my fist into your fat gut!"

"Uh...listen Ralph, I lost my temper and got desperate. Calm down. We'll work something out," Bob said, not sounding as confident as his words.

"Oh? Tell me how we're going to work it out? The cops already have an APB out for your home invasion, taking hostages, and attempted murder of four people. And here's a news flash — Chuck's going to live and you know what that means? He'll tell the cops everything. My unit is already searching for me. I'm hiding out in Keyes. Where are you?"

"I'm not saying. You'll come over here and beat on me." Bob's hands shook when he heard Ralph grunt into the phone. His big cousin was pretty scary in a temper. "If only Aunt Clara had left my uncle's teardrop to me after she died, none of this would have happened. I told that dumb lawyer 17 years ago it should have gone to me, but he wouldn't listen. Said Aunt Clara left everything to Mary and I couldn't do a thing about it. Just because my snooty sister loved going to those stupid gatherings with our aunt and uncle. They were all a bunch of jerks."

"You shouldn't speak ill of the dead, Bob."

"Why not? Mary, her husband, my aunt and uncle all thought they were too good for me."

"Quit your whining and think for a change."

"I am. Like I've been telling you for years, before my sister and her husband died in that car crash, she admitted Aunt Clara's teardrop held the answer to our family's hidden treasure." Bob ground his teeth. "Then she took pleasure in telling me that the trailer and everything in it, including the urn holding Uncle Richard's ashes, and a key, were lost in the flood. But she wouldn't tell what the key opened and what else was hidden in the teardrop. We have to get to that trailer. The answer's in there."

"So, what's your plan? I know mine. Find the money or whatever it is and get out of Dodge."

"Don't worry, Ralph. I figure that annoying duo won't give up on their research. I'm keeping tabs on them, from a distance, of course. I figure they'll do the work for us by taking the teardrop apart until they find our missing piece. Then we strike."

Ralph grunted again. "You better make sure you keep your distance until you know for sure. We don't have much time, remember," he said before ending the call.

* * *

Amy ran out of the bedroom when she woke to find Jerry gone. "Jerry! Jerry! Where are you?"

"I'm out here, honey," he answered.

She sprinted into the garage. The teardrop's door, some of its siding and the fenders lay on the garage floor. Jerry's feet stuck out from under the trailer. She bent over and looked at him. "Jerry, why are you tearing our teardrop apart?"

"I'm glad to hear you still refer to it as ours because I definitely feel the same. Bob is not getting it. Even if he asks nice this time," Jerry said, his voice muffled.

"But why are you tearing it apart?"

"Looking for anything that might tell us what he wants so desperately. And don't worry, I'll put it back together once I...ouch!" Jerry rubbed his head as he slid out. Pieces of weeds covered his T-shirt and hair. "Amy, where'd you go?"

"I'm over here. You know, we never looked inside this ice chest. I don't know why. Maybe because it seemed so ordinary."

Jerry stood and dusted himself off. "Go ahead and open it. I'm done searching here. Didn't find a single thing. Oh, and I called work, and after telling them what happened, they said to take the rest of the week off. What about you? Did you call?"

"No, but I will. Jerry, come over here."

He went to the other side of the teardrop. "What's up?"

Amy held out a small book. "I found this under a piece of cardboard in the ice chest and ... it looks like another diary, a newer one."

Jerry's shoulders fell. "Oh, I thought maybe you found a stash of diamonds or something."

Amy scanned the pages. "This may be better than diamonds. I can understand everything written here. It's not old and tattered like the other one they stole. A different woman wrote this. The writing's not the same." She gasped when she got to the last page. "Jerry, this last entry is dated."

"Oh, yeah, what's the date?" Jerry tried to look interested, but he didn't think another diary would help much.

"January 1997."

Jerry sucked in a breath. "Whoa, now we're

talking."

They hurried into the house, avoiding their shot-up couch to sit at the kitchen table.

"Wait a minute while I call work. Then I'll read this page out loud," she said.

"My ears are waiting, so make it fast."

When she returned, Amy took a couple of deep yoga breaths before beginning.

January 1997

I can't believe we found it! It's a cave right by the river. The map was true, just like my beloved Uncle Richard had told Aunt Clara it would be. It's on someone's private property, but luckily no one's around. We pulled my aunt's teardrop, mine now, down here with our Jeep. We'll be spending the night. Wish the weather was better. We've had nothing but rain and more rain since before New Year's.

It's comforting to know Uncle Richard's ashes are with us while we uncover my family's hidden treasure. And here we all thought it was just a family legend handed down for generations. No one knew Aunt Clara and Uncle Richard kept the old map hidden in their teardrop all this time. I'm honored she picked me to find this secret spot. Though we're not sure what's in the cave — money, gold perhaps?

Aunt Clara knew I'd share whatever it was with the family, unlike Bob and his greedy soul. He's not speaking to me and I consider that a blessing. I'm tired of being bullied.

We didn't bring enough supplies and are

heading out in the Jeep before we get started with our treasure hunt. We've unhooked the teardrop. Won't be gone long, it'll be fine. And then we'll open that cave's rusty iron door with the key.

As soon as Amy finished reading, Jerry jumped up and raced back to the garage.

"Hey, wait for me." Amy held tight to the diary as she ran after him.

She found him staring at the teardrop. "Where do you think they'd hide a map?"

"Guess it would depend on how big it is."

Jerry scanned the side of the trailer; stopping at the rubber-lined cap Andreas had said wasn't standard. "See that cap? Do you think the map could be hidden in it? Would have to be small and thin."

"Well, what are you waiting for? Take it out."

"OK, let me see if I can pull it off." The cap wouldn't budge. "Amy, could you get me a screwdriver from the work bench?"

"Coming right up."

She ran back with the screwdriver. "Hurry; the anticipation is killing me."

"I'm trying," Jerry grunted as he twisted and pried on the cap with the screwdriver. Finally it popped off, landing on the garage floor.

"Bingo!" Amy pulled a rolled piece of animal hide out of the cap. "Oh, it's old and a bit cracked." She unfurled it carefully. "Holy cow, look at this, Jerry. It's like a Treasure Island map. You know, pirates searching for a buried chest."

"Let's see that," Jerry said, taking it from Amy. His heart thumped as he looked down at an inked drawing of a river with dots pointing to a riverbank with a sheer cliff. At the bottom of the cliff a door was drawn into the rock like the entrance to the cave Mary described in her diary. The writing was small and hard to read. "Amy, you still have that magnifying glass you use for your stamp collection?"

"Yes, I'll go get it. Meet me in the kitchen where the light is better."

"OK." Jerry's knees wobbled so much he could hardly walk. They'd found the missing piece. Unbelievable.

The magnifying glass helped them make out the name of the river and the town in which the cave was located — the Tuolumne River in Hickman.

"That explains how the teardrop ended up in Tuolumne River Park. The 1997 flood must have washed it downstream for miles," Amy said.

Jerry, still peering through the glass, said, "Hmm, the cave won't be that easy to find. We wouldn't be able to get to it by car, like Mary did. She must have known the area really well. The road she took might not even exist any more after the flood." Jerry sat up straighter. "But if we went on the river, we could travel downstream and scan the shore."

Amy laughed. "Right. Like we're actually going on this treasure hunt." She studied the back of the map with the magnifying glass. "Oh, boy. Look at this, there's a date —1870. Wasn't that the year the urn was stolen?"

"Yeah, it was. Weird, huh?"

"You know what's even weirder?" She pointed to the corner of the map. "Look at that."

Jerry squinted through the glass, spotting two tiny Rs in a mirror image, just like on the urn. "Wow, this is getting more and more interesting."

Amy pushed away from the table. "I think this whole thing is getting way too creepy."

"I'm calling Mario at work," Jerry said, tapping out his friend's number on his cell.

"Hey, buddy, do you still have that canoe? Yeah, yeah, I know you asked me a dozen times to go canoeing, but I never had the time. Do you think we could go on a little jaunt down the Tuolumne on Saturday? Like maybe launch the boat at Roberts Ferry and go downstream to the Waterford Bridge?"

Amy waved her hands wildly at him. "Jerry! What are you thinking?"

He put a finger to his lips, shushing her. "I know this is a weird request coming from me, but I'll explain when you pick me up. So, will Saturday about 9 work for you?

"Great! Thanks buddy, see you then."

Amy's face grew red hot. "You are not getting in a canoe to search for that cave. You know how you hate being on the water. What if you fall in the river and drown? You can't swim worth a darn. And besides all that, you can't take someone else's family treasure. It wouldn't be right."

"I'll be fine. Mario won't let me drown. And I'm not keeping Mary's treasure. I just want to see what all the fuss has been about. Serve Bob right if I find it first. I'll turn it over to the authorities and they can find the owners of the treasure."

"What about me and Tracy? Are we supposed to sit home and worry about your fool heads?"

"No, you'll be our pick-up. After we unload the canoe, you, Tracy, and Bianca can take Mario's SUV and go have breakfast. Then meet us at the Waterford Bridge. Simple, right?"

"Simple, my eye. This whole scenario sounds dangerous and crazy. What if Bob and Radcliff are at the cave?"

Jerry waved the map in her face. "Who has this?"

Amy slapped it away.

"Hey, be careful. This is very old."

Amy grumbled, trying to think of more reasons to stop Jerry. Sure, it'd been fun researching the teardrop's history and finding the map, but that was the end of the treasure hunt. She couldn't let Jerry take this risky trip, on a canoe no less.

"Maybe there's nothing in that cave. Or it could be haunted or cursed."

Jerry rolled his eyes. "Come on, Amy. You sound like Andreas. It'll be an adventure. Get into the spirit. We need to finish this mystery we've spent so much time on."

Amy got a smug look on her face when she thought of her final argument. "You don't have the key to open the iron door. I'm sure Bob has it now. So what would be the point in finding the cave? A total wasted trip."

Jerry grinned. "Nice try. No worries on that score. The door to the cave is probably so rusted it'll fall in when we push on it." He leaned over and kissed Amy on her tightened lips. "Easy peasy, sweetheart."

CHAPTER THIRTEEN
Girish Parikh

Mario came over to Jerry's house Friday night with the canoe so they could prepare for the next day's adventure. The two men were very excited, but Amy was worried. "I don't know what will happen to you," she said.

"Wish us luck, Amy," Jerry said. "We won't have to work for the rest of our lives if we find the treasure." He sounded as if he had changed his mind and now wanted to keep whatever they found.

But after Mario left, he didn't sound so confident. "I don't know how this is going to go. We could even die!"

"Don't say that," Amy said in a soothing voice. "You'll get back just fine." Jerry pulled her close and they snuggled, taking comfort in each other.

* * *

The next thing she knew, Amy was snatching the

map from Jerry's hand. "I don't want you to go on that damn trip!" she shouted.

"Amy, honey... the treasure..."

"I don't want someone's treasure."

Exhausted now and not knowing what to say, Jerry lay back on the bed and fell asleep, the map held tightly in his hand.

As he entered a deep sleep, the map dropped from his hand and fell onto the table near the bed.

When Amy heard it fall, she leaned over, put it in a dish she used for candles and set it on fire. She couldn't believe what she'd done. She gathered the ashes into a pile and stared at them in horror. What have I done, she thought. Why did I do this? Jerry will kill me!

As she looked down with tears in her eyes, she saw that the pile of ashes had turned into a dazzling diamond!

Amy's body jerked, and her eyes flew open. It had all been a dream, an incredible dream. But was it an omen?

The map was right there on the table. She touched it. Yes, it was real.

Late that night, a small red truck passed Jerry and Amy's house. Bob looked nervously at the house as he drove by.

"Bob, why is there a canoe parked in front? Is that the right house?"

"Ralph, what's wrong with you?" he answered. "Yes, it's the right house."

"But that canoe . . ."

"I don't care about the canoe. We have the key to the treasure, but we don't have the map," Bob said.

"It must be in the trailer," Ralph said. "We've got to get it before that nosy couple does."

In the morning, Mario came to Jerry's house and brought Tracy and Bianca with him. Amy tried one more time to get Jerry and Mario to give up their plan, but the two were adamant.

She sank into a chair, her face in her hands. I don't care if they don't find anything, she thought. Neither couple was rich, but they were living comfortably on what they earned. Just let Jerry and Mario stay safe.

This terrible trio has disrupted our lives, she realized with a start. To her, the trailer, urn, and diary were just that, even though Jerry would call them a terrific trio.

There's no use fighting them, she thought. Instead, I'll join them.

"Okay, what do you want us to do?" Amy asked the guys.

"Glad you've come around," Jerry said. "We've worked together on this mystery, and together we can solve it. Let's focus on the treasure."

Jerry and Mario studied the map again, and after some discussion, Jerry said, "This is what we will do: You three drop us off at Roberts Ferry Bridge. Then we'll launch the canoe and start the treasure hunt."

"We'll give you a call to pick us up when we're done," Mario promised.

And with that, they were off. It took about 40 minutes to reach the covered structure just off Highway 132.

Amy, Tracy, and Bianca left Jerry and Mario near the river with hugs all around. The plan was to pick them up at the Waterford Bridge, several miles downstream.

Amy and Tracy sat talking at Cathy's Coffee Shop in Waterford, while Bianca sipped her apple juice. Suddenly, Amy flashed on what Andreas had said to Jerry in their garage. It had struck her at the time to the point that she'd scribbled his words on a piece of paper, then tucked it into her purse.

Now she started fumbling for the paper.

"Did you lose something?" Tracy asked.

"Tracy, Andreas, our neighbor, said this to Jerry: 'Are you documenting everything you are doing? You know, if the person in that urn is famous, like Jimmy Hoffa, you can make millions selling your story.'"

"I'm not a writer," Amy continued, "but if you like the idea, you and I can write the story of our adventure. Who knows? It may make some money. Maybe not 'millions,' but something. I should have kept a diary, but the events are still fresh in our minds. The title can be Treasure in a Teardrop."

"I like that idea," Tracy said. "Yes, we have a story."

"It's intriguing; it could even make an exciting movie. Let's keep our project a secret, a surprise," Amy said. Tracy nodded.

"Fiction or nonfiction?" Tracy asked.

"I'm not sure, but I know it's a mystery," Amy said.

"I wish Hitchcock were alive," Tracy said. "In *Psycho* a car sinks in quicksand. And in our story, an almost sunken trailer kicks things off," Tracy said. "I have an idea," she continued. "Let's make it a mysterical story!"

"What's that?" Amy asked.

"It's a story that combines mystical elements in the mystery — mysterical. Do you like it? I just coined the word."

"We should dedicate the book to Andreas, Jerry, Mario, and Bianca," Amy said.

"Why Andreas first?"

"He planted the idea to write the story," Amy answered. "And above all, he saved our lives."

"Let's go to the library and borrow some books on how to write a mystery," Tracy suggested. "Don't worry, Amy, our story will be good. It may not win the Nobel Prize, but we will be proud of it."

"I hope so," Amy said.

"Just keep daydreaming, girl," Tracy said. "Who knows? It might lead to some interesting plots. But let me warn you, Amy. Some writers have told me that writing can be addictive."

"So we're going to write a book, make money, and we've gained a trailer, too," Amy said with a laugh.

"Yeah, we can pack it with books, and Jerry and Mario can tow it to distribute the books on weekends."

"Not so fast, Tracy," Amy said. "We've still got a lot of unsolved pieces, such as the mystery surrounding the Brewsters and McHenrys, and the diary and the baby. And don't forget Chuck, Bob and Deputy Radcliff. That will provide plenty of suspense. Of course, the biggest unknown is whether Jerry and Mario find the treasure."

* * *

"Jerry, enjoy the water without getting wet, OK?" Mario said. "Put on your life jacket. This is your first time canoeing and you don't know how to swim. I hope this fits you," he continued, tossing the orange flotation device at him.

Then Mario proceeded to give Jerry a crash course on canoeing, demonstrating how to paddle. "And here are some water shoes," Mario said.

"What are water shoes?" Jerry said.

"You'll understand if we have to land on a rocky shore to reach the cave. These shoes will make it easy to walk. Amy told me your size and I bought you a pair."

"Mario, you are also a treasure," Jerry said and the friends broke into laughter.

"That's not all. I've got wide-brimmed hats with straps to protect our heads, sunglasses, a camera, and a cell phone in a waterproof bag."

"We'll also need this water so we don't get dehydrated, and a bailing bucket in case the canoe capsizes," Mario said.

"Yes, boss!" Jerry shouted, shuddering a bit at the thought of ending up in the water.

Mario told him that the front part of the canoe was the bow and the back was the stern. He showed him how to get into the canoe and move to the front. Then Mario moved to the stern and they were moving.

The Tuolumne was full of wildlife. In a matter of moments, they saw an eagle, a hawk and some ducks.

The canoe moved past farms and gravel pits, but no sign of any cave. They were getting frustrated when they spotted a hole at the bottom of a cliff. They paddled the canoe to the shore and got out. As they neared the hole, they could see that an iron door was attached to the opening.

They were tugging on the door when they heard a voice.

"Hi buddies," Bob shouted.

CHAPTER FOURTEEN
Bridget Foster

Jerry jumped at the sound, his feet slipping on the pebbles.

"Easy," Mario said, steadying his friend's arm.

Bob and Radcliff sat near the shore in an aluminum fishing boat. The deputy angled it upriver and let it drift back toward a willow tree while Bob leveled his Glock at them. "Just stay where you are," he said.

Like we're going anywhere, thought Jerry. There were about three feet between the bottom of the cliff and the river. They could hardly make a jump for the boat — canoe, he corrected himself, as Mario had been doing all morning. He looked over at him, moving only his eyes, afraid to move anything else. They had avoided disaster today but had come close a couple of times when Jerry was first learning how to row.

Watching Radcliff negotiate the boat, Jerry blurted, "I thought you couldn't have motorboats on the river."

"So sue us. Now sit tight while we get organized." Bob glared at Radcliff, who ignored him and went about tying the boat to the tree.

Jerry continued to stare at Mario, hoping he was formulating a plan. They hadn't thought to bring a weapon. A shovel and a pick were in the canoe, which was just out of reach. Jerry had a brief sense of déjà vu, remembering Amy's fears the night before about the trip. He hoped she would get the chance to tell him "I told you so."

"How'd you find us?" Mario asked.

"Not hard when you're working with a cop," Bob said. "We planted a tracking device in the canoe last night then just motored on down when you stopped." His voice smacked of satisfaction. "Now don't get any ideas. The good deputy here is going to get out and open that door."

Radcliff was edging his way along the thin strip of riverbank toward them.

"I see you brought some tools with you. Perfect. You, Jerry's friend, get them out of the canoe." Bob motioned with his gun for Mario to go over to the canoe.

Mario climbed carefully back in just as he had taught Jerry. He sat down in the same place he had been earlier, with the knapsack between his feet.

"Now, hand the tools to Jerry," Bob said from the motorboat.

Jerry took the three steps over to the canoe and Mario handed him the shovel, followed by the pick.

He set them against the cliff, next to the entrance to the cave. He tried to see up into the cave but the stout iron door covered it completely. The entrance was set up the cliff a couple of feet, and you could tell by the watermarks that the river didn't usually rise that high. He wondered how high it had gotten during the flood that had washed the teardrop trailer downstream.

"Okay, you two, you know I am not afraid to use this, so just do as you're told," Bob said, pointing the Glock directly at them. "Radcliff, you go in first and scout it out."

The deputy pulled a small LED flashlight out of a cargo pocket on his pants and walked up to the door. It was secured with a heavy chain and padlock. "Need the bolt cutters."

Keeping the gun leveled on Mario and Jerry, Bob hopped out of the motorboat and walked toward the cave with the tool. Radcliff snapped the lock easily and climbed into the cave. Jerry saw Mario slip something out of the knapsack and into his pocket while Bob's back was turned.

"Get over there with your friend," Bob ordered Mario. "Here is how we are going to do this. You two are going to be our labor, so thanks for bringing all the tools. Radcliff has a gun, too, so don't get any ideas about being heroes."

The deputy jumped down out of the cave just then. "It's farther back than I thought, but there's a door back there, too. This one has a keyhole. Give me the key, and I'll open it."

"Hold your horses," Bob said. "You keep an eye on these guys and I'll open the door. One step at a time, partner, one step at a time." Bob motioned Jerry and Mario away from the entrance, then stuck the gun in the back of his pants and climbed into the cave.

Jerry tightened his hand around the pick, but a nudge from Mario stopped him from lifting it. His friend nodded toward the deputy, who had just drawn his gun. Jerry thought that if he really were a hero, he would pick up one of the baseball-sized rocks at his feet and bean Radcliff with it while Bob was in the cave. But he'd never been much of a baseball player, and getting shot wasn't on his to-do list today.

Bob jumped out of the cave, startling them. "OK, I unlocked the door. Ralph, go back and get the lantern set up. I'll follow with these two. Looks like we have some digging to do, and this may take awhile. X does not mark the spot."

Jerry and Mario climbed into the cave with the tools, followed by Bob, who kept back far enough to be out of shovel range, his Glock at the ready.

The floor of the cave was gravelly and sloped up toward a cleft in the rock. Light emanated eerily from the back, where Radcliff had set the lantern. Jerry noticed that it wasn't dry as he expected. Water trickled down the walls in places, and there was a damp, moldy smell. When they got through the cleft, a room-sized space opened up. The remains of a fire pit were in the middle, and trash littered the floor. One of the walls was painted with graffiti and a couple of lewd words.

"Jeez, you'd think people would have more respect," Bob said, glaring at the debris. "This place could have some historical significance. OK, there's the door. Get going."

An alcove in the back of the cave was portioned off with an iron grate; part of it swung open. It reminded Jerry of the old iron jail cell that still sat in Knights Ferry. Maybe they were fabricated at the same time. Radcliff stood just inside the entrance, the lantern hung up on the bars. Mario started through the grate, dragging the shovel with a look of determination on his face. Again, Jerry hoped his friend was coming up with a plan for their escape because he sure wasn't. His only other thought so far had been to swing the pick at Bob when he wasn't looking and grab for the gun, but he figured the odds of that working were poor.

"Radcliff, where do they start digging?" Bob asked from behind them, poking Jerry in the back with the gun.

"I don't know, could be anywhere." Radcliff stood in the middle of the twelve-foot space, scraping the floor with his boot as if he were looking for something.

"What's back there?" Bob asked, pointing the gun toward a narrow space in the back of the grotto.

"Keeps going, gets real narrow, though," Radcliff answered. "Probably ends at some point."

Bob walked to the back of the alcove, pacing out

the length of the room as he went. Then he turned and measured the width. He pointed at a spot in the corner opposite the grate. "Dig there."

Jerry and Mario looked at each other, then got to work. Mario swung the pick to loosen the rocks and Jerry scooped them out with the shovel. They had dug a hole about a foot deep when Jerry paused and looked at Radcliff, who was standing over them with his gun.

"So what are we looking for?" he asked.

Radcliff looked at Bob, waiting for his response.

"Let's just say we will know it when we find it," Bob said.

"So you don't know what it is?" Jerry seemed surprised that these two masterminds weren't bragging about what they expected to find.

"I didn't say that."

"So what is it?" Jerry asked again. Mario just kept digging.

"Yeah, what is it?" Radcliff echoed.

Bob stared at them, like he was trying to decide what to say. "OK, what the hey. You won't be around to tell. What is it they say? Dead men tell no tales." He chuckled to himself. "This has been a family secret for more than 100 years." He paused for a couple of beats to draw out the suspense. "It's gold. Civil War gold."

"Civil War? What would it be doing out here?" Jerry asked.

"You're not a history buff, are you?" Bob reached into his pocket and pulled out a pack, then shook a cigarette loose. He struck a match against the sole of his boot and lit up, settling back against the wall, getting himself into storytelling mode.

"During the Civil War, Northern California sided with the Union and Southern California went with the Confederacy. Some went back to fight and some supported the war effort in other ways. There was a lot going on in California then. Ulysses S. Grant was even stationed in Humboldt before the war. You probably know who he was, right?"

Jerry stopped digging and leaned on his shovel. "Of course."

"Keep digging," Bob said in a gruff voice. Taking a pull on the cigarette, he watched them dig for a bit, then started talking again. "Yeah, old Ulysses had a sister in Knights Ferry. Bet you didn't know that. Anyway, when it looked like the South would lose, the Confederacy took all of its gold out of the Treasury and decided to hide it so the Northerners wouldn't get it. They put it in different caches around the countryside, planning to go back for it when they needed it. Well, it was war, you know, so some of it disappeared."

"What, it was stolen?" Radcliff asked.

"Not everyone is as honest as you would like them to be," Bob said.

That's ironic, coming from a man pointing a gun at us, Jerry thought.

"Anyway, family legend has it that some long-lost cousin was part of one of these treasure-trove details and got a hold of some of this gold. Hid it out here after the war."

"So this is all just a legend? You don't even know for sure it's here?" Jerry asked, wondering why the cousin or some other family member hadn't been back to retrieve it by now.

"It's here. Keep digging." Bob tossed the cigarette butt and ground it into the damp earth with his heel.

Turning back to the hole, Jerry and Mario worked into a kind of rhythm. The thump of the pick and scrape of the shovel were the only sounds except for the constant drip, drip, drip of water. Jerry was just about to ask for a break when his shovel hit something that looked different.

"Big rock here," he said. "I don't know if we can go any farther." Jerry leaned on his shovel handle, stalling for time so he could catch his breath.

Mario looked into the hole, a funny look on his face. "Let me see that shovel."

He scraped away some gravel, then squatted down and used his hand to clear more. "Looks like concrete."

"What?" Bob walked over and looked into the hole, waving the gun at Jerry to back away.

Radcliff peered over the three of them, trying to get a look. Jerry thought now would be a good time to try and get away but even if he made it out the door without getting shot, he doubted his friend could.

"It looks old," Mario said.

"What is it?" Jerry asked, curiosity overcoming his fear.

"See if you can break it up with the pick," Bob told Mario. He stepped back, gun in hand.

Mario lifted the pick over his head, getting ready to take a big swing at the patch of concrete. He slammed it down as hard as he could and the concrete crumbled. He swung again and it fractured further. His third blow punched a hole in the slab. The tip of the pick hit air this time. Mario used the pick to pull up a chunk of concrete, revealing a dark space underneath. "It would help if we had a pry bar," he said.

"There's one in the boat. I'll go get it," Bob said. "Keep your gun on these guys."

Mario used his hands to scrape more of the gravel off what they now could see was a square of crumbling concrete. Jerry moved in to help him, both of them squatting in the hole.

"When Radcliff goes down, get his gun," Mario whispered.

Jerry stiffened, not sure he had heard correctly. He saw Mario slide something pink out of his pocket and palm it. Jerry moved gravel around with his hand, clueless as to what the hot pink object was. He didn't know what Mario would do, but he was fairly sure that Bob had no intention of letting them get out of there alive.

"Hey, Radcliff, can you give us a hand here?" Mario asked, his head down and hands out of sight.

"Just wait for Bob," the deputy replied.

"I think I can see something down there. Bring

your light." Mario motioned over his shoulder with his other hand.

Radcliff pulled the flashlight out of his pocket and leaned over the hole. "Let me see."

Mario spun from his crouched position and jabbed the deputy in the thigh with the pink object. Radcliff's eyes bugged out and then he went stiff, jerking a couple of times before dropping the gun and falling to the ground.

Jerry jumped out of the hole and scrambled for the gun, which slid across the gravel. He grabbed for the barrel as it came to a stop against a rock. Radcliff was still twitching on the floor when Jerry stood up, fumbling to point the gun at him.

"What is that?" he asked Mario.

"A taser. Tracy carries it with her when she runs in the mornings. It's a special one for girls."

"Seems to work for boys, too. Now what?" Jerry held the gun in front of him with shaking hands.

"Only other way out could be back there," Mario said, pointing to the opening in the rock.

They were looking at the back of the grotto, where a tunnel headed deeper into the cliff, when they heard Bob's voice.

"OK, let's get at it," he said as he walked into the grotto, pry bar in one hand, gun in the other at his side. As soon as Bob was through the door in the grate, he saw Radcliff on the ground. "What the hell!" He turned toward Mario and Jerry, pulling his gun arm up.

Jerry took one look at Bob's gun and pulled the trigger on the one in his own hand.

CHAPTER FIFTEEN
Clyde V. Collard

Jerry's shot missed Bob, struck the rock wall and ricocheted. Bob shot wildly twice, spun and scrambled out of the cave then ran for the boat. Jerry crawled after him and got out as Bob was already scudding downstream. Jerry raised the pistol and sighted at Bob's receding back. He hesitated then dropped his arm. "Nope," he said aloud. "I don't want to kill anyone."

He turned and shouted back into the mouth of the cave, "OK, Mario. Drag Radcliff out of there."

"Are you kidding?" came the reply. "Get down here and give me a hand."

Jerry ducked back into the cave and grinned at the sight of Mario poised over the fallen Radcliff with a rock in his hand.

"Well, we got one of them," boasted Mario.

"Yeah, one out of two ain't bad."

Once they had dragged the stunned Radcliff into the open, Mario looked at the small canoe and shrugged. "We still got a problem."

"Yeah, that dinky canoe will never hold three."

"What'll we do?"

"One of us will have to go back for a motorboat and since you're better than me, you will have to go," Jerry said. "I suggest that Bob is long gone but just in case I'm wrong, you take the gun with you."

"What about Radcliff?"

"We'll tie him up and if he makes a move I'll conk him with a rock."

"How come we're both so cool after this?"

"Beats me. Maybe because we drank our Ovaltine. Get going."

* * *

"I knew it! I knew it!" Amy was on the verge of tears. I told you not to go out there on the water."

"I didn't drown, I was shot at," Jerry remonstrated.

"That's even worse. Now where are we?"

"We're out of it, that's where we are. No more map, no more treasure, and no more shooting. We have reported this latest episode and put everything in the hands of the police. Let them handle it. That's what we pay them for."

"And no more getting rich," a note of regret crept into Amy's voice.

"That too," agreed Jerry, "but it was all sort of a game to begin with and a pipe dream to the end."

They gazed quietly at each other, savoring a

poignant moment of shared feelings until the ringtone broke their reverie.

"Is that you or me?" asked Jerry.

"That's you, dummy. Who else would have that Lone Ranger tiddy-rump, tiddy-rump, tiddy-rump-rump-rump theme?"

"Okay, Tonto, I'll give you that one. He took the iPhone from his jacket that was tossed on the sofa. "Hello? Yes, speaking. (Pause.) Yes, we can do that. (Pause.) Okay, ten o'clock. Yes, we'll be there." He rang off.

"Well, who was that?"

"Police," Jerry said. "They want us to come down to the department at ten o'clock tomorrow morning. I told them we would be there."

* * *

The tall, older man in the dark blue suit exuded an aura of authority as he smilingly welcomed each of the three couples into the lounge of the Modesto Police Department.

"Please be seated," he said, "and make yourselves comfortable. I have asked you to come here today because you are the three couples touched by this teardrop trailer confusion and I want to explain the intricate nature of the often terrifying situation in which you have found yourselves. With us today is Captain Jonathan Spencer of the Modesto Police Department." He motioned to the uniformed officer standing near the window. "My name is Orson Wright. I am an agent of the Federal Bureau of Investigation."

"The FBI?" gasped Amy.

"Yes, Mrs. Curtis, the FBI. The federal government is involved because the underlying events in which you were entangled include federal offenses. However, before I expand on that point I wish to congratulate Mr. Curtis and Mr. Smith on the bravery they displayed in a difficult situation and their ability to get out of a tight corner relatively unscathed.

"Having said that, and though I hate to disillusion you, I want to tell you that all of you were on a wild goose chase. The map was a phony, the key meant nothing, and there was never a Confederate treasure. There was a very different kind of treasure that was connected to your finding the trailer and the decorative urn. It is a convoluted story that began before most of you were born, with the exception of Mr. Andreas Stavros. If you will bear with me patiently, I will explain the circumstances leading to your involvement.

"One day before Thanksgiving in 1971, a man identifying himself as Don Cooper, later to be known as D.B. Cooper, boarded a Northwest Airlines 727 with a bomb in his satchel. He commanded the pilot to land in Seattle, where he demanded two hundred thousand dollars in small bills and two parachutes as ransom for the release of the passengers. His demands were met and the plane flew away south with a minimum air crew. Sometime later, though still above the state of Washington, Cooper put on a parachute and dived out of the rear of the airplane. Though he was sought for many years by experienced trackers, Don Cooper was never again seen alive."

"Yes, sure," said Jerry. "I think we all know the story of D.B. Cooper. What has that got to do with us?"

"Be patient, Mr. Curtis. All will become clear. But now I would like to go back before Cooper's exploit and show how the social setting of the 1960s contributed to your present problem of the urn in the teardrop trailer. This was a tumultuous time with the Vietnam War, civil rights, peace movements, feminist rights, hippies, and the march on Washington. But the most devastating was the tremendous rise in criminal activities. And, during that time, one of the most virulent criminal groups in America came to be known as the Ninth Street Gang."

"Ninth Street," gasped Amy. "You mean right here in Modesto?"

"Right here in Modesto," averred Wright. "Ninth Street south of the river was worse than many of the big-city criminal enclaves of Prohibition days. Drugs, robbery, holdups, prostitution, mayhem and murder. You name it. And the leader of that most vicious gang was none other than Bob Barr's Auntie Clara. Clara Barr made Ma Barker seem like a Sunday school teacher. She had a hand in all that went on in the den of iniquity that was Ninth Street. Don Cooper and his kid brother, Pete, were members of Clara's gang and without her knowledge they cooked up that hijack scheme. After Cooper escaped with the money, he couldn't get back to Modesto so he thought up the urn idea. He stuffed the money into the urn, clamped a seal over it and filled the upper cavity with ashes stolen from a local mortuary. Then he shipped the urn off to his brother. When Pete Cooper received the urn his first thought was to hide the money before Aunt Clara found out about it. He did get it hidden but shortly after, Clara killed him and dumped his body in the river.

"Apparently she was aware of the brothers' plot all along and had chosen her own time to do something about it. That was when she concocted the story of the Confederate treasure. She remembered a cave along the river where she used to hide illegal contraband long before she drew the gang around her. She had a map drawn up showing the location of the cave as the spot where the treasure was buried. She hid the map in the trailer and the key in the urn. Mary's so-called diary was also a fake. Mary was one of the toughest members of the gang; like aunt, like niece."

"But why?" interjected Andreas Stavros. "Why would she make up such an elaborate scheme? How would it profit her?"

"Times were not good and law enforcement was cracking down. The men were restless and wanting some activity. Bob and Ralph were especially loud in protest. Bob was the most vicious member of the gang; you will notice all the shooting was done by Bob. He was also ambitious to take over the gang which, of course, would mean eliminating Clara. She knew this and the major reason for the treasure fraud was to keep Bob and the other men involved in something that would distract them from any thought of deposing her. They had the map and the urn with the key. But after the urn was lost with the trailer, most of the gang lost interest in the game. But not Bob and Ralph. Then, when the trailer was recovered they felt their luck had changed and got right back into the hunt.

"Now here is where it gets tricky." Wright moved over to put his hand on the urn, which stood on a low table.

"All the fuss over a paper and a diary and a map supposedly revealing the site of the treasure, when the map was staring you all in the face. You all thought the etchings and sparkly things were decorations but they were more than that. Look at this mosaic pattern. See the squiggly lines and curvy lines and hatch-marked lines? You don't have to be a cartographer. Anyone who is familiar with the county should be able to go right to the treasure. The curvy line is the Tuolumne River, these heavy crossing lines are major streets; Yosemite to the north and Hatch Road to the south with the river in between. This picket fence line is the Santa Fe Railway. And south of Empire, that dot right here is the spot where Pete Cooper buried the money from the Northwest hijacking."

Wright put the tip of his index finger on the small crossbar.

"X marks the spot," he said.

Jerry jumped up from his chair, protesting in an angry voice, "What a cock and bull story. Nobody knows what happened to Cooper and if it was him, why ship the money down here in the urn? How do you know he stole the ashes? Who invented the kid brother? And that yarn about Aunt Clara. Who writes your stuff, anyway?"

"You're right, Mr. Curtis. There is much surmise and conjecture in that story. There are things we will never know and questions we will never have answered. But there is also solid evidence, reliable observation, and tattle-tale stories from involved witnesses."

"Yes, dear," said Amy, reaching for Jerry's hand. "Sit back down and listen. He's not trying to fool you with a fabricated story."

Jerry sat down, still scowling and shaking his head.

"All right, Mr. Curtis," said Wright. "I'll explain some of the sources of knowledge on which this tale is based. Part of it comes from reliable, trained agents who have observed the participants for many years. Part of it comes from projections of highly probable factors following one another. And finally, the most factual parts come from eyewitness accounts of those personally involved in the action."

"For instance?" Jerry was still not mollified.

"For instance, highly trained and experienced federal agents; for instance, analysis by professional diagnosticians; for instance, Chuck Addis and Ralph Radcliff," Wright rattled off the background.

"The Ninth Street Gang is defunct. In 2001 Aunt Clara died in a fire on Ninth when the motel they were using as gang headquarters caught fire and the blaze swept through all the structures. The Coopers were already gone and the few remaining members vanished into the woodwork. Cousin Mary is doing a long stretch in the Women's Facility at Tehachapi.

"When the gang was at its peak Ralph and Bob were just kids but they saw and heard most that went on. Much of the story I outlined came from Ralph's memories. Bob is dead. Ralph had a hideaway in Keyes and after you frightened him off," a nod to Jerry, "he went to the Keyes hideout. The police were hot on his trail and when they tried to arrest him he chose to shoot it out and they killed him. However, Chuck has recovered and telling everything he knows and Radcliff is singing like a canary.

"That about wraps it up. The Cooper money was recovered from a plot in a pet cemetery on Santa Fe Road where Pete Cooper's pet German Shepherd, Regal Rex, was buried, hence the RR on the urn. We recovered 180,000 dollars and Northwest Airlines is giving a ten percent reward which will go to you, Amy and Jerry.

Eighteen thousand is not too bad. It's all yours and the urn."

"No, no," said Amy. "Half goes to Mario and Tracy."

"Whatever, it's yours to do with as you please."

Slowly the tension began to dissipate as the three couples thanked Mr. Wright and, chattering excessively, trailed out of the room.

"Boy, that's over . . .

"Let's go home . . .

"I don't like that . . .

"How about Andreas . . .

"I still don't understand . . .

"Aw, forget it . . .

"We still have the book to do . . .

"What happened to the . . .

"Talk about nothing . . .

"Thank God!

As the quiet settled on the room Captain Spencer grinned at Orson Wright, "I think Curtis was right . . . that was some cock and bull story."

"Yeah, but the question remains, who was the cock and who was the bull?"

MEET THE AUTHORS

Micheal Maxwell was raised in Modesto with family roots dating back to the 1880s in Stanislaus County. He attended Stanislaus Union School, Grace Davis High School, Modesto Jr. College and CSU Stanislaus before receiving his Master's Degree from Chapman University in Orange, CA. *The Cole Sage Mystery* series is published on Amazon Kindle. He's also the author of *Three Nails*, and is included in the Mystery/Thriller Anthology, *Eight the Hard Way*, published in the UK.

Kent L Johnson holds a BS in Biology, one patent, and he worked in the agricultural sciences for over twenty years. Kent, at one time a road warrior, traveled all over the world and numerous places in North America where he managed to see distinct cultures first hand, eat and drink, and drink some more from expense reports that mirrored fine fiction in their ability to deliver a theme capable of full reimbursement. Kent has completed three novels, all in the editing stage, and many published short stories.

Louise Kantro, who retired from teaching English at Modesto High School in 2012, received her MFA in Creative Writing from Goddard College in 2003. Since then, she has published poetry in *Quercus Review, Song of the San Joaquin,* and *Poet's Corner*, and was featured in the regional poetry anthology, *More than Soil, More than Sky.* Her short stories, creative nonfiction, and poems have been published in journals from all over the country. Recently she became a member of the National League of American Pen Women.

R. Garrett Wilson was born and raised in California's Central Valley. He has a Masters of Software Engineering from Penn State University and currently works as a programmer/analyst. Garrett enjoys reading, writing, photography, and woodworking, and belongs to the Fresno Science Fiction and Fantasy Writer's critique group. Some of his stories have been published in *Analog Science Fiction* and Fact and FSFW's 2010 anthology, *I Dreamed a Crooked Dream*.

Jennie Bass was born and raised in Modesto, California, where she has spent all but five years of her life. Although she enjoys teaching high school math, she has a deep appreciation for the written word. Jennie is a First Degree Black Belt in Taekwondo, and has published one book, a contemporary romance titled *Year of the Dog*, under the pseudonym Kat Madigan.

Alexandra Deabler is an aspiring freelancer writer currently working at *The Modesto Bee* newspaper. She recently moved back to the Modesto area after living in Boston for a year where she survived a hurricane, a blizzard, and a bombing. She graduated from the University of California, Davis in 2011 with a BA in English literature. In college, she made the Dean's List and had an essay she wrote on King Lear selected to be presented at an annual Shakespeare event. She writes short stories and comedic personal essays for her blog, www.alidoesthings.com.

Julia Washington is a Modesto native currently working on a Bachelor's Degree in Creative Writing with a concentration in Fiction at Southern New Hampshire University. By day she works as a Director of Volunteer Services for the Area Agency on Aging. She has assisted in projects with "You're Us, Sankofa Theatre Company" and now the Stanislaus Reads and Writes Community Novel. An avid blogger, Julia is eager to finish her education so she can devote more time to her blog www.californiadarlin.wordpress.com.

Dana Ardis never goes anywhere without a book and a pen. She grew up reading a generous mix of literary classics, science fiction, and fantasy. This has probably done something irreparable to her brain. She's been to eight countries on three continents and keeps track of such things on a map in her art studio. She currently works at the Stanislaus County Free Library in Modesto, surrounded by books. It's a perfect fit. Find her on Twitter @zooluki or at danaardis.com.

Tally Scully has spent the last decade working in high-end California nurseries. Tally has been a member of the Modesto Garden Club since 2010, serving as Director of Internet. Tally recently co-penned with her niece *Houdini and the Magic Molt*, an educational children's garden adventure story that was illustrated by her mother. She is enjoying sharing the story with elementary school students through presentations. In her spare time, Tally loves to boat, garden, and hike with her husband Mike Scully.

Ellie Cummins, a writer of fantasy fiction and paranormal romance has been obsessed with anything that makes her heart flutter. From vampires and monsters to regular humans—she loves to write about extraordinary beings that bring a level of something good, even though the odds are stacked against them. She is currently signed with Keith Publications awaiting the release of three books and can hardly wait to set her characters free inside the minds of those who read about them.

Doug C. Souza's favorite genres are science fiction and fantasy, but he enjoys a good yarn of any variety. His story "Mountain Screamers" will be published in *Asimov's Science Fiction* magazine this summer. Other works have appeared in numerous anthologies and ezines. As a member of the local writers' Meetup group, he helps aspiring writers find their voice (and possibly a paycheck) for their work. Doug C. Souza teaches fourth grade in Modesto, California where he lives with his wife (and main reader/editor) Nicole. Find him at dougcsouza.com.

Loretta Ichord has five published non-fiction middle-grade books with Millbrook Press/Lerner Publishing. Four are in a series called, *Cooking Through Time: A history of American food from colonial times to the present.* The fifth book is *Toothworms and Spider Juice: A history of dentistry for kids.* Two of these books were placed on the list of Notable Social Studies Trade Books for Young People. Loretta lives on an almond ranch with her husband Bill. She's the mother of four grown children and grandmother to five. Find her at loretta-ichord.com or on Twitter @LorettaIchord.

Girish Parikh is an award-winning author and journalist based in Modesto, California. He writes prose and poetry in both English and his mother tongue Gujarati (the language of Gandhi.) His latest book in English is *The Day of Gloom and Glory!* He is also the author of several other books including seven on computer software.

Bridget Foster was a columnist for ten years, has contributed numerous articles to education publications, was editor of a reference collection of online resources for H. W. Wilson and has just completed her first novel, a mystery set in a northern California ranching community. A former teacher and administrator, she now works in the education technology industry with companies in the US and Europe. She resides in Knights Ferry and spends her free time at home on the ranch with her family and numerous horses, dogs, and cats.

Clyde V. Collard, a native Californian and graduate of Livingston High School experienced a wide variety of industrial and scientific occupations in his youth. He received two degrees from San Jose State University before earning his doctorate in sociology from Louisiana State University. He spent 30 years in education and was a professor at California State University, Stanislaus for 20 of those years. As an academician he wrote and published in his chosen field for many years before turning his literary skills to the realm of fiction. He has published four books.

Made in the USA
San Bernardino, CA
04 October 2014